THREE IMAGINARY BOYS

A HALLOWEEN STORY
IN THREE ACTS

Also by J.T. Holden

Fiction
The Whiter White House
True Son
Apple-polisher
JB: Or The Unexpected Virtue of Being Swaggy
(also published as *The Curious Disappearance of JB*)
The Boys From Manchester

Poetry
Alice in Verse: The Lost Rhymes of Wonderland
Twilight Tales: A Collection of Chilling Poems
O the Dark Things You'll See!

THREE IMAGINARY BOYS

A HALLOWEEN STORY
IN THREE ACTS

J.T. HOLDEN

KURO
黒

ISBN 13: 978-1-937696-15-3 • ISBN 10: 1937696154

First Edition

To Baumer & Hasney
for inspiring the story

To Marilyn
for inspiring the storyteller

Deep inside
The empty feeling
All the night time leaves me
Three imaginary boys

—The Cure

CONTENTS

ACT ONE
IN THE BEDROOM

A T FIRST, IT WAS DARK AND QUIET.

Then Logan said, "Hit that light, would you?"

Drew flipped the switch by the door and looked around. It was a fairly large bedroom, neatly organized and spotlessly clean. He looked at Logan, who was at the window, closing the blinds. "So, what are we doing? Do you have a script?"

Logan shook his head. "Nah. We're just gonna ad lib it."

"What's the scene about?"

"Just two guys in a room. One guy invites the other guy over to his house after school to help him out with a drama class project, and we'll just take it from there."

"So it's just two guys in a room doing a scene about two guys in a room?"

"Uh-huh."

"What're our names?"

"You'll be Drew, and I'll be Logan." Noting the look in Drew's eyes, he elaborated: "It's simpler to use our own names, and it'll make it feel more natural."

Drew nodded, though he still looked a little dubious. "So, what? We're just playing ourselves?"

"Basically, yeah. We're two guys who've seen each other at school. We've never hung out or anything, just nodded to each other in the halls, maybe said hello a few times. But other than that, we don't really know each other. Then my character gets this assignment to do a scene for his drama class—only he's one warm body short, and there aren't many prospects. Then he sees you outside after the final bell and figures, 'What the hell—he's breathing, right?'"

Drew's jaw flexed, and his cheeks burned, but Logan didn't seem to notice. He was busy adjusting focus on the video camera that stood on a tripod next to the bed.

"And so," Logan continued, "he comes up to you and asks if you'd help him out with his scene for drama class . . . which *is* a bit odd because other than an occasional 'Hi' in the hall or 'What's up?' in the cafeteria, he doesn't even know you exist." Logan offered a small apologetic smile, though his eyes seemed to convey a different sentiment. "No offense."

Drew didn't look offended this time; he just nodded like it was all good and said, "So, in a way, the scene already started before we got here."

"Now you're getting it."

"So we're actually still doing the scene right now."

"Yep."

Drew took a measured breath and said, "So, what's the camera for?"

Logan looked up from the camera's viewfinder with a shrewd eye and said, "We have to document the scene."

"What about before, when you came up to me after school?"

"What about it?"

"You said the scene had already started before we even got here, right?"

Logan nodded, but he seemed more concerned with the camera than with Drew's question.

"So, why didn't you document our conversation back at school?"

A moment of silence passed.

Then Logan raised an arched brow and said, "What makes you so sure I didn't?"

There was no hint of guile in Logan's calm gaze, no teasing smile playing at the corners of his mouth, but Drew sensed bravado and rolled his eyes.

While Logan continued to adjust the camera's settings, Drew turned his attention to the collection of karate trophies that lined the shelves across the room. The row of shelves was flanked by two glossy wooden wall racks. One held an assortment of bo staffs while the other displayed a collection of swords, including a katana whose deadly blade gleamed under the dim light.

Still eying the display of weapons, Drew said, "So everything we're saying here is just part of the scene . . . which is interesting, at least from my perspective, because I've never done anything like this before . . . and I'm not trying to slam your idea or anything like that, but do you think an *audience* would really find this interesting? Or that they'd just get bored? Not at your idea," he hastened to add, "I'm not saying that—it's actually a pretty cool idea—but more at me, because maybe I'm not really that interesting, you know?"

He was fishing, but Logan wasn't biting, and so he changed tack.

"I mean, most people are looking for something more interesting than just two guys in a room talking, you know?"

"Maybe," Logan said, as he continued to adjust the camera's focus. "But if you have a contrast between the two guys it can be *very* interesting. That's why I picked you. Granted, it's not really all that original, but it's a good starting point for conflict: brain versus brawn, intellect versus instinct, academic versus athlete, whatever labels you prefer."

Drew smiled wryly. "So, I take it you're the brain."

Logan shrugged, pulling focus in careful increments as he continued to watch Drew through the viewfinder. "One of us has to be the smart guy."

Drew nodded, but his tone was petulant. "So, I'm the dumb jock."

"I didn't say you were dumb."

"No, but wouldn't it be implied since you're obviously the academic smart guy?"

Logan looked up from the camera and said calmly yet pointedly, "Well, I *did* get you to come here."

The flicker of doubt in Drew's eyes was more than enough for Logan to feed on, and he stood up straight and spoke with a bluntness that was almost too convincing.

"Let's at least be honest here. All I had to do was tell you what a good actor I thought you'd be, compliment your build, tell you that you're the best looking guy in school and that all the girls are dreaming about you, and you were following me home like a lost puppy. That's what makes you so right for this scene. Everybody at school thinks you have a huge ego—and, let's face it, you do—but the thing they *don't* know is just how *insecure* you are. They don't know the depth of your desire for reassurance and approval. *That's why I picked you. You're a natural.* Your strength is in your weakness. You *are* a dumb jock . . . but you're not stupid."

Drew shook his head. "Yeah, whatever."

Logan said, "Are your feelings hurt?"

"Nope."

"You sure about that?"

Drew's cheeks flushed again, and his nostrils flared sharply. He looked at the wall of trophies and said, "So what do you want me to do?"

"You're already doing it," Logan replied simply.

"Right."

It was quiet for a moment.

Then Logan broke the silence. "Are you pissed?"

"No," Drew said instantly; then just as quickly, though twice as sharply, he snapped, "NO!"

Logan was unmoved by the outburst. Drew released a slow, calming sigh, but his cheeks still burned, and the muscles in his jaw were tense.

The tone of Logan's voice remained infuriatingly reasonable. "It just seems like you're a little pissed."

"Is that where you want this scene to go, with me getting pissed?"

Logan shrugged. "Wherever it goes, it goes."

Drew shook his head, looked around the room again, and said, "So, do you want me to do some push-ups, flex my muscles, dumb jock-like things?"

Logan pondered for a brief moment. "Actually, that's not a bad idea . . . "

Drew's eyes narrowed.

Logan elaborated. "It would certainly give you a more plausible incentive to have come here in the first place."

Drew gave a short laugh. "What? To do push-ups and flex?"

Logan shook his head. "No. To *model*. We'll say my character is an artist who needed a model for his art class project, and so, obviously, he chose you."

Drew's eyes narrowed again. "I thought it was a *drama* class project."

"It still is," Logan said with a smile. But Drew's gaze remained wary.

"What about all the stuff we've already done? The scene about the two guys doing a scene for drama class? This is like a whole new scene . . . so what, are we starting from scratch now?"

"Nah," Logan said, "it's the same scene. It's just taking a slight turn. It starts with me asking you to come over to my house after school to help me out with this drama class project, which, once we get here, you discover is a scene about two guys doing a scene for a drama class project . . . then after the setup, it shifts. Your character makes a joke about taking off his shirt and flexing . . . "

"I didn't say I was gonna take my shirt off."

Their eyes locked, but Logan had the advantage.

"I think it would be *implied*," he said shrewdly, "that within the context of your offer to pump and flex, you'd be taking off your shirt, don't you?"

Drew remained silent. Logan pressed on.

"Now, *within* the scene about the two guys doing a scene for drama class, *my* character gets a *new* idea and wants the scene to be about a guy who's an *artist* who gets this dumb jock guy to come over to his house so he can take pictures and draw sketches of him for his art class . . . it makes more sense when you think about it, considering he'd have a much easier time convincing the dumb jock to come over and model for him than he would to have him help out with an acting class project, don't you think?"

Drew's cheeks flared crimson, and there was no disguising the sarcasm in his response. "Yeah, 'cause the dumb jock probably wouldn't be able to remember all the dialogue for a scene anyway."

"Pages of expository dialogue, with a twist that even *I* couldn't see coming," Logan nearly cried with a chuckle of delight. "Fuckin A, brother. It's like art imitating life imitating art. That's why the scene was set up to be ad-libbed in the first place. But when *my* character realizes that *your* character doesn't even have enough brain power to handle something as rudimentary as *that*, he shifts the project to this modeling-art class thing . . . "

Drew's cheeks flushed deeper, and the edges of his nostrils flared nearly white. Logan's cool grey eyes shimmered as the ghost of a taunting smile played at one corner of his mouth.

" . . . which works right into the whole scene perfectly, because now Abercrombie Boy really *is* getting pissed because Genius Boy is hurting his feelings."

"You're not hurting my feelings."

"You sure about that?"

"Positive," Drew said, but the muscles in his jaw continued to flex. "It's not like we're friends."

"Exactly," Logan said, pointedly. "So why are you here?"

"You asked me."

"And who am I to you?"

Drew's eyes iced over. Logan waited patiently for his response.

"Nobody," Drew said pointedly.

"That's right," Logan said, taking a step closer to Drew, challenging him with his gaze. "I'm *nobody*. I'm *nothing* to you. But I don't remember you hesitating for a single second when I asked you to come over and help me with this thing. I thought you'd puss out, but you didn't. Now, why do you suppose that was?"

Drew shrugged, but his jaw remained tight. "Didn't have anything better to do."

"Wrong, Jethro. The reason you came over here is the same reason you're not heading for the door right now. Do you know what that is?"

"Do you want me to go?"

"Do you want to go?"

Drew's nostrils flared again, but he averted his gaze when he spoke. "Can we just do the scene?"

Logan said, "We *are* doing the scene."

Drew shot a glance at Logan, then turned his gaze back to the trophies, debating his next move. After a measured moment, Drew spoke without taking his gaze off the trophies. "Do you want me to take my shirt off?"

When no response came, Drew peeled off his T-shirt and tossed it aside. Then he took a deep breath and turned to face Logan. There was a brief flicker in Logan's eyes, just enough to let Drew know that Logan was impressed.

Drew knew that he had an impressive physique, and he certainly wasn't blind to the daily glances he received from his peers, both male and female. There was this one kid, a skinny freshman named Matt Saesan, who liked to take secret pictures of Drew with his phone when he thought Drew wasn't looking. The kid had even taken a few shots of Drew in the locker room after gym class, which, to Drew's surprise, hadn't really bothered him. He knew what Matt Saesan was going to do with the pictures, but instead of being grossed out by the thought of the kid rubbing one out over a picture of him fresh from the shower, Drew was actually flattered.

But even more flattering—and infinitely more *satisfying*—was that flicker in Logan Kōtarō's eyes. Even though this was only a scene for a drama class, and Logan had warned him in advance that he was going to say and do things to put him on edge, Drew couldn't suppress the sliver of satisfaction that rose within him. Somehow knowing that his body had impressed this smug prick with his shelves of trophies and his perfect GPA was like a victory for Drew . . . one that ended abruptly the moment Logan opened his mouth.

"Do you have to wear that thing all the time?"

Logan nodded at the pad that looked like a circular bandage on the lower left side of Drew's stomach. A thin, clear tube ran from under the pad to the little black box clipped to Drew's belt. Drew looked down at the circular pad affixed to his stomach and fell instantly back into character.

"Do you want me to take it off?"

Logan shook his head. "I was just wondering if you had to have it on all the time."

"No. It's just convenient."

"What do you do, just push it once after you eat?"

"It depends on what I'm eating."

"What if you push it by accident?"

Drew shook his head. "Nothing." A short beep sounded as he pushed the button on the box. "It's just a little dose each time."

Logan's gaze became thoughtful. "Did you ever O.D. on it?"

"Not to the point where it was really gonna hurt me," Drew said. "I think I hit it a couple too many times at work once, and I had to eat a candy bar to counteract it."

"What'd it feel like?"

"I got a little woozy."

"Did you faint?"

"Nope." Drew sighed. "So, is this gonna be a scene about two guys talking about diabetes now . . . that could create some real tension . . . or are we sticking with the modeling thing? 'Cause if we are, I should probably take this off. I don't think the guy would be modeling with a tube coming out of his stomach."

Logan was still looking at the pad when a sly grin began to curl. "I kind of like it," he said. "It makes you seem less . . . invulnerable."

Drew smirked. "So, I'm invulnerable now. What am I, Superman?"

"I was thinking more along the lines of Captain America . . . but Superman *did* have his Kryptonite."

Drew rolled his eyes. "I think we're getting off the track here."

"I think we're dead on the money."

Drew gave a curt nod. "It's your scene."

"It's *our* scene," Logan corrected.

Drew looked around the room, chewing thoughtfully at the corner of his mouth. "So, do you have a sketchbook?"

"What for?"

"The 'art class' project that you asked me over here to help you with. I think it would be *implied*—within the context of the scene—that you would have a sketchbook."

"Yes, it would . . . *if* in fact I had invited you over here to help me out with a project for *art* class—which I didn't. Within the context of the scene, as you put it, my character shifted the project from drama class to art class. But in fact, we're still in the middle of the original scene, which is still two guys doing a scene for drama class."

"Which makes no sense at all."

"It got you to take your shirt off."

"Which ties into the scene how?"

"By revealing your Achilles heel," Logan said with a wink and a nod at the insulin box clipped to Drew's belt.

"Which makes no sense either," Drew said with a labored sigh.

"Which makes perfect sense if I didn't invite you over here to do a scene at all."

Drew froze. Logan's eyes appeared to teem with sparks.

"What if," Logan said carefully, "'within the context of the scene,' Smart Guy invites Jock Boy over to his house to help him out with a drama class project, which he then shifts to an art class project, which he only does to get your guy to take his shirt off and reveal . . . his little box of concentrated Kryptonite . . . "

"Which still doesn't make any sense," Drew said flatly. But his voice faltered, and Logan could see the uncertainty in his eyes, the seed of apprehension blooming within.

"Which makes *perfect* sense," Logan said, "*if* the smart guy didn't invite the dumb jock over to help him with a class project at all."

Logan's hand came from behind his back and hung easily at his side; held in his grasp was a gun.

A long silence followed, in which Drew's Adam's apple rose and fell in dreamlike slow motion. Logan had said nothing about a gun when he'd given Drew the setup for the scene outside of school.

"It makes sense," Logan continued in a reasonable tone of voice, "if the whole class project thing was just a ruse the smart guy used to lure the dumb jock over to his empty house for a little after-school revenge. Not very plausible on the surface—I mean, he hardly knows the guy, right? But no more implausible than a guy who doesn't know the first thing about acting agreeing to help a complete stranger with a drama class project, and we both know how that one turns out, don't we?"

"What do you want?" Drew said forcefully. But the fear behind his hard gaze crept through, and Logan, who had not expected this level of commitment or intensity from a guy like Drew, could not deny that he was impressed.

Logan took a silent breath, allowing the moment to simmer. Drew's Adam's apple bobbed again, and his chest began to rise and fall as the thoughts behind his eyes moved dangerously fast. Feeding on the palpable tension, Logan took it up a notch.

"What do you suppose it would take for someone to set a trap like that for a guy he doesn't even really know?"

Drew shook his head—a scarcely perceptible movement—and croaked, "I don't know."

Logan said, "Make an effort."

Drew stuttered, "He'd have to be . . . he'd have to be pretty screwed up."

"Maybe he doesn't need a motive," Logan said, thoughtfully. "Maybe he wasn't even sure he was going to do it in the first place . . . but then after the ball gets rolling, he just wants to see how far he can take it."

Drew looked at the gun again. He didn't know much about firearms, but he knew that it was a revolver and that it held six bullets. It had a brushed nickel finish, and it was the scariest thing he'd ever seen in his life. The fact that the gun was dangling easily at Logan's side instead of pointed at him did nothing to ease Drew's fear.

Logan was as tall as Drew, though not nearly as broad. With his sharp Eurasian features, long lean frame, and dark shiny locks overhanging his brooding eyes, Logan Kōtarō looked like a live-action version of one of those anime characters on Adult Swim—the sort of guy who concealed a chiseled body under his clothes and knew precisely how to use any number of the weapons on the wall racks behind him. Drew had seen Logan with his shirt off in the locker room at school and could vouch for the fact that the guy indeed had a carved body, and the collection of karate trophies at the center of his weapons display indicated that Logan was more than capable of defending himself. And yet Drew had never thought of Logan as a physical threat. Until now.

The gun, whether pointed at him or not, changed everything. With Logan's training in the martial arts, it wasn't difficult for Drew to imagine just how quickly Logan would be able to raise the gun and get off a shot—possibly even several shots—before Drew could come close to bridging the distance between them. And even if Drew could get to him before Logan had the chance to raise and fire the gun, he suddenly wasn't so sure he could take Logan in a fight. He'd seen massive guys taken down by much smaller guys on *Ultimate Fighting Championship*—and all of those smaller guys had one thing in common: they all had the same look in their eyes that Logan Kōtarō had right now—the look that promised they would fight to the death.

Logan's fingers curled around the gun's butt, and his forefinger grazed the trigger, as if he could read Drew's thoughts. Drew looked back into Logan's eyes and waited. Logan took a pair of handcuffs from the back pocket of his jeans and tossed them to Drew, who instinctively caught them.

"Put them on, please," Logan said.

Drew swallowed hard, tears suddenly forming in his eyes as he looked at the cuffs in his hands. Logan's gaze was calm yet unyielding.

Drew said softly, "Dude, I'm begging you . . . "

Logan snorted a humorless laugh and said, "Dude, I'm begging *you*."

Drew searched Logan's eyes, but there was no remorse or pity in them.

A long moment passed, and Logan waited patiently. Then Drew secured one of the cuffs around his wrist and was about to secure the other when Logan said, "*Behind* your back, please."

Drew's lips parted, but no words came out. After a brief hesitation, he secured the loose cuff around the other wrist, pinning both of his hands behind his back.

"Now," Logan said calmly, "turn around and get down on your knees."

For an odd moment, Logan felt certain that Drew was going to rebel—a scintillating notion that sent a wave of tendrils racing his spine. But then the hard look in Drew's eyes faded and was replaced by an almost poignant desperation. As Drew got down on his knees, a deeper thrill raced through Logan, the sort he'd last felt nearly seven years ago when he was a boy. But he wasn't a boy anymore. He was a seventeen-year-old young man now, and his control of *this* situation was infinitely more assured. He crossed the carpet soundlessly and pressed the muzzle of the gun against the back of Drew's neck as he squatted to check the handcuffs. As he'd suspected, they were a little loose. He couldn't blame Drew for trying—after all, the scene was designed to allow for a little improv—and he gave a slight smile as he tightened both cuffs snugly around Drew's wrists with satisfying clicks.

"There we go," Logan whispered close to Drew's ear. "Nice and snug. Just one more little modification and we'll be ready."

Drew's mind was racing frantically now, but he held it together on the outside and managed to ask, "Ready for what?"

"You'll see," Logan said as he rose and clapped Drew on the shoulder. His hand remained there for a moment, squeezing reassuringly. Then it slid away, and there followed the sound of a drawer opening and closing. Drew wanted to turn his head to see what Logan was doing, but he resisted the temptation.

Logan came back from the dresser with a braided belt and immediately wrapped it around Drew's ankles, cinching it tight. Then he looped the loose end of the belt around the chain of the handcuffs and tied it off securely.

"Almost there," he said, clapping Drew's shoulder again and squeezing a little harder this time. "Don't go anywhere. I'll be right back."

When Logan walked away, Drew couldn't resist turning his head to look. He saw Logan at the door, and for a moment, he thought Logan was going to leave him alone in the room. If that was the case, Drew felt almost sure that Logan wanted him to escape, or at least attempt to escape. It was still a scene they were doing here. It had taken an unexpected and spooky turn with the gun and the handcuffs, but it was still just a scene for a drama class project. And Drew couldn't help thinking that if Logan was about to leave him alone in the room, he more than likely wanted Drew to escape his bonds—perhaps even wait behind the door for Logan to return and flip the tables on him. It was just a scene, Drew reminded himself, and how much farther could they take it like this?

He geared himself up to break free. Logan would have hidden the key to the handcuffs somewhere nearby. Or maybe they were trick handcuffs with a secret unlocking button that didn't need a key. Either way, he needed to be ready to make his move the moment Logan left the room.

But Logan didn't leave. He simply stood at the door, listening for a sound from the hallway outside. When nothing came, he locked the door and returned to Drew, crouching down, so the two of them were eye to eye.

Drew worked to hold his own under the pressure of Logan's gaze, but the fear within refused to recede—he just couldn't get the unexpected appearance of the gun out of his mind. Only after Logan had lowered his gaze was Drew able to relax. And even then, only for a moment.

A chilly wave of tendrils raced over Drew's body when the muzzle of the gun grazed his stomach and then caressed his skin in high looping arc and a downward swoop—if there was any doubt in Drew's mind what this meant, it was vanquished when Logan pulled the gun back briefly before tapping Drew's navel with the muzzle, as if placing a discreet dot below the invisible question mark he'd just drawn.

Their eyes met again, and Logan was impressed with the palpable fear that Drew exuded. He made a short brush-stroke along Drew's stomach with the muzzle of the gun, as if underlining the circular pad affixed there, and asked, "Is it a small needle, or a big one?"

Drew swallowed back the rising lump in his throat, trying to remember. When it finally came, he forced himself to respond. "It's a small one."

"Can you feel it poking you?"

Drew shook his head.

"So small and thin it's like it's not even there, eh?"

Drew nodded, unable to take his eyes off of Logan's.

"So you can take it off whenever you want."

Drew nodded again. Logan smiled pleasantly.

"I think we'll leave it on. OK?"

Drew scarcely nodded this time. Logan released a soft sigh, as if pondering an innocuous question. Then he looked down at the little black box clipped to Drew's belt, and his eyes gleamed with mild curiosity.

"What would happen if I pushed the button?"

Drew swallowed again. "It would give me a dose of insulin."

"Would it hurt you . . . if you didn't need it?"

"No."

Logan pressed the button, and a short, soft beep emit-ted from the little black box. He looked up into Drew's eyes, as if mildly surprised—and a little amused—at the sound of the beep.

"What if I hit it again?"

Drew remained silent. Logan pressed the button again.

"I mean, how many hits would it take before it started to have an effect on you? Two?"

Another beep sounded off.

"Three? How many times did you hit it that time you got woozy?"

"I don't remember—" Drew began, but before he could finish, the next beep cut him off.

"Was it four?"

Drew swallowed back the fear that had reached an entirely new level—the level that Logan wanted to see. But still, some part of Drew's mind cried out for him to hold it back. It wasn't time to reveal his fear—not the full thrust of it, anyway, not yet.

"I'll bet it had to be pretty scary, whatever it was, eh? How full is this thing right now?"

Drew remained silent. Logan pressed on from a different angle.

"If you took like half of it at once, without having any candy or soda to counteract it, would it put you in a coma?"

Drew scarcely managed a nod.

"So, how many shots are in a vial? Ten? Twenty? There'd have to be more than that, right? What? Thirty? Forty? More than thirty, right?"

Drew didn't know, but he nodded again, anyway.

"So, like five or six wouldn't do that much, right?" Two more beeps sounded off, and Logan released a short laugh. "You'd probably have to lose count altogether for it to have an effect."

A quick double beep, followed fast by another beep, and Drew's hands clenched into fists behind his back.

"I think you got the point—" He swallowed hard. "I

think you got the point across. If you're trying to scare me, you're doing a pretty good job of it . . . 'cause I'm getting pretty scared here . . . OK?"

Logan nodded and responded softly, "OK."

A brief moment passed.

Then another beep sounded.

Drew closed his eyes and began to take measured breaths, his chest rising and falling with each one.

Logan watched in fascination, as if Drew's fear were sustenance and he, Logan, a starving soul with an unquenchable appetite. He was about to press the button again when something unexpected happened.

From the hall outside his room, a voice called out: "Logan? Are you home?"

Drew's eyes opened at once and shot to the door, but before he could do anything, Logan pitched the gun onto the bed and grabbed a bandana from the night table. As Drew opened his mouth—whether in protest or to call out for help, he did not know—Logan shoved the bandana between his teeth and quickly tied the loose ends tight at the back of his neck. Then in one swift movement, Logan snatched the gun off the bed, pressed its cold muzzle to the underside of Drew's chin, and cocked the hammer.

Drew froze in fear. *Real* fear.

Logan spoke in a deadly whisper: "You need to understand that I'm an insane person, and though she is my sister and I love her dearly, I will not hesitate to kill her, because I could not bear to see her burdened with the knowledge of what I am. I would rather see her dead than exposed to a single *glimpse* of that darkness. And if I kill *her*, then surely my anguish will spill onto *you*, and I swear to you on all that I hold sacred, the rage that will follow will make this little scene we've been playing look like a lovely dream by comparison."

He paused to give Drew the full effect of his steely gaze. Then he continued urgently in that same deadly whisper. "It is not my intention to kill or even harm you. I merely wish to incapacitate you for a brief time so that we may share an unforgettable moment of release together. Though my mind is clearly unstable and my thoughts are mostly a jumble of incoherent memories colliding in a sea of confusion, my heart is true, and my intentions toward you are mostly innocuous—save for the passion that drives me to conquer and control you. Give me back but an ounce—a single *drop*—of that same passion and I will pledge my soul to you."

He pushed the muzzle of the gun deeper into the shelf of Drew's chin, and his eyes shone darkly.

"But if you scorn me, know this: my name is Wrath, and I will *burn* this earth—and all that I care for on it—to exact a slow and excruciating vengeance upon you."

Drew trembled as he stared into Logan's eyes. Though it was only a scene—it *had* to be, this couldn't be happening for real—some part of him believed every word that Logan had said. Though he was confused and had no idea why Logan had suddenly started speaking like a Shakespearean villain, spewing threats of biblical proportions, some part of him believed that if he made any attempt to deviate from the current path of the scene, it would be a dreadful mistake, one from which there would spring very *real* consequences.

The longer he gazed into Logan's dark eyes, the more woozy and disoriented he felt. Not from the insulin box— that would have been impossible, because it wasn't even his. Logan had put the pad on him and clipped the little box to his belt before they'd started the scene. He'd watched Logan remove the needle beforehand—and even if Logan had somehow been able to sneak the needle back onto the pad, surely Drew would have felt it poking into his skin, no matter how small and fine it was. Perhaps the feeling of wooziness was from the adrenaline racing wildly through his body—he'd never done anything this intense before in his life. Perhaps he had just fallen so deeply into the scene that he was overdosing on whatever it is the brain produces that makes real actors seem so convincing in all those movies and TV shows. Regardless, he felt like he was high on something and was in no shape to offer any resistance, and so he remained perfectly still and quiet.

He was still looking into Logan's eyes when a sudden sound gave him a jolt. It was the girl who'd called to Logan from the hallway outside the room. She was knocking on the door now, and her voice, closer yet still muffled, came from the other side: "Logan?"

"Yeah, what?" Logan called back in a perfectly natural tone of voice.

"Are you gonna be here for a while?" the girl asked.

"Yeah, why?"

"I have to go, and I'm not gonna be able to feed the dogs at six. If you want, I can feed them now, but you'll have to take them out before you leave, 'cause I'm going out with Gretchen, and I don't know when I'll be back."

"I'll feed them at six and take them out."

"Well, don't forget, 'cause Mom won't be back until late, and they'll crap inside if you just feed them and don't let them out, OK?"

"OK. I won't forget."

All was silent for a moment. Then came the sound of footsteps fading down the hall. Then from the foyer downstairs, the front door closing, and shortly after, the sound of a car engine firing up in the driveway below Logan's bedroom window.

Then Logan looked at Drew with a conspiratorial grin. "Macy is spending the night at Gretchen's, and Mom won't be back until late." His grin deepened, but his eyes looked mournful. "Looks like we've got the place all to ourselves."

A moment passed.

Then a single beep cut through the silence, and for a long while, it was dark.

From the darkness there came three sounds.

The first came from someplace outside Logan's bedroom window—an eerie sound that sent a wave of goosebumps racing over Drew's body, but it was only the wind passing through the eaves and sending a shower of leaves scraping down the side of the house.

The second came from inside the room—a familiar and comforting sound that made Drew thirsty, it was the pop-fizz of a can being opened, followed by the bubbly splash of its contents pouring into a glass.

The third also came from inside the room—a familiar sound, though not exactly comforting; it was Logan's voice. Close by and pitched low, it cut through the silence like a cool blade slicing through a tender nerve, like the voice of someone particularly adept at telling ghost stories at sleepovers and around campfires.

"I want to show you something," Logan began in a tone just above a whisper. "I need to show you something, so that you may understand what has happened here tonight . . . what is yet to be, but doesn't have to be, because this is still *our* scene, and we can shape it in any form or direction we please. Do you understand what I'm saying?"

Logan paused, and in the silence that followed, Drew could hear the slow throbbing of his own heartbeat, the pounding pulse of blood crashing in his eardrums. He felt drained and a bit woozy, but that was just part of the scene—he was *supposed* to feel that way, and so he went with the feeling and fell deeper into the trancelike moment, allowing himself to be lulled by the sound of Logan's voice in the darkness that surrounded them.

"The first thing you need to understand," Logan went on, "is that everything goes in threes, and that this is only the beginning. There are still two more acts to come. But even so, you must believe that *we* are in control, that we shape our own scenes. Even when the script has already been written, we always have the power to control our own scenes *within*. Like when you agreed to come over here to help me with this project. That was *your* choice. Nobody put a gun to your head—not at that point, anyway. You came of your own free will. Do you follow me? Do you understand that?"

He paused again, though he did not expect a response. Then he went on in that same oddly soothing tone.

"*We* can make decisions, like the one you made to come here today, because *we* are still alive. And as long as we are alive, we can choose our own paths. Only the dead have to abide by the rigid rules of the script. And we're not dead. We know this because we can still feel fear, while the dead fear nothing.

"Fear is not our enemy. Fear is good. Fear keeps us from

going into that house where the windows are all dark . . . it keeps us from climbing those stairs to the shadow-streaked hallway at the top . . . it keeps us from that door that stands open—just a crack—at the far end of that hallway. And though we are curious, we do not need to see what lies beyond that door. We need to turn away and run back down that hallway for the stairs. And we cannot stop. We cannot look back. We need to bolt down those stairs and race from that house, and never look back, because there are things beyond that door at the end of the hallway . . . things far worse than death . . . and, trust me, you would not care to witness these. I will do anything I can to spare you from what lies beyond the door at the end of that dark hallway. But I need you to help me. I need you to see what I see . . . and I need you to *fear*."

He paused again and listened to the sound of Drew's labored breathing. Time was running out, and he knew that he would have to make a move before Drew slipped away . . .

. . . *into a coma. If I slip into a coma, I could die . . .*

The sound of those words, echoing back through the long and winding corridors of his memory, sent a wave of chills racing up Logan's spine.

Just make sure to stop before I slip into a coma, OK? You need to make sure that you give me the soda to bring my levels back up. Do you understand?

Logan understood very well. He would not make the same mistake twice.

But he had to be sure that *Drew* understood.

Logan looked off to the low-hanging moon outside his bedroom window and shivered. As the curtains swayed in the breeze, he placed a hand on the back of Drew's neck and pulled Drew close enough that their foreheads were touching.

"I need to show you something," Logan whispered in a dry voice. "I need you to see and understand that I have only done what I've done to protect you. I need you to believe this, and I need you to run from that house . . . run from *me*." He uttered a choked sound, like a sob. "I need you to know that I could have killed you tonight . . . I was going to kill you . . . to save you from that room at the end of the hall . . . I was going to do that for you." He swallowed back another sob and gritted his teeth. "But instead, I've chosen to give you the fear. The *gift* of fear. The fear that will keep you safe . . . "

He pressed his forehead closer while tightening his grasp on the back of Drew's neck.

"Can you *see* them? Can you see them standing at the top of the stairs? Do you understand what they want? Do you understand that they want you to join them in the room at the end of the hall? Do you understand that once you go in, you can never come out?"

Drew shuddered. Logan held him closer. Time seemed to stand still.

Then Logan's voice came again, rising to a harsh whisper.

"Can you see the three boys? Can you see them standing there at the top of the stairs? Do you understand what they want from you? Do you understand that they will do whatever she tells them to do? Do you understand that? Are you afraid now, Drew?"

He could feel Drew's body trembling fiercely, but he waited for the response. He *needed* the response.

And momentarily, it came.

Drew nodded as a hot tear spilled slowly down his

cheek. Logan breathed a sigh of relief. Then he placed a hand beneath Drew's chin and, with a gentle movement of his thumb, brushed the tear away.

He took the gag from Drew's mouth and brought the glass of soda to his trembling lips. As Drew drank, Logan looked again to the moon outside his bedroom window, and in his smoky grey eyes there gleamed a sharp edge of defiance—an icy glare of insolence, born of an unjust punishment—and, if only for that fleeting moment, it made him feel strong and true.

He waited for Drew to drain the glass before setting it on the night table. Then he loosened the belt around Drew's ankles and unlocked the handcuffs.

As he rubbed Drew's wrists and arms to get the blood circulating again, he spoke in a soothing tone. He told Drew that everything was all right now, that it was just a scene and that he had done a good job, and that he appreciated Drew's help with the drama class project. He did this carefully, so as not to disturb the seeds he'd planted in Drew's mind—the fear that he wanted Drew to carry with him as he skulked off into the night.

He wanted the memory of the scene to linger so that the next time Drew saw him in school, he would offer no more than a wary nod of acknowledgment before turning away and heading in the opposite direction.

He wanted it to end here, with no second or third acts. He wanted this more than anything. But after he'd seen Drew to the door and watched him drive off, the moon was still there, hanging low just outside his bedroom window, waiting for him.

And later still, as he lay alone in the dark, trying not to look out the window, he could feel the thrumming beat of his own heart, the accelerated flow of the blood coursing through his veins, and he knew that it wasn't over. He knew this because he understood that everything, whether real or imagined, always comes in threes. He had known this since a time he cared not to remember.

He had completed the first act, and inevitably, two more would follow. His resistance might hold for a while, but eventually the moon would change his mind.

He pulled the covers up high and buried the side of his face in the pillow. But it didn't do any good. Even with his eyes tightly shut, he could still see them. The three boys. Like sentinels, patiently waiting for him.

Only this time, they weren't at the top of the stairs.

This time, they were standing in silent silhouette by the low-hanging sliver of the new moon just outside his bedroom window.

ACT TWO
UNDER THE MOON

A T FIRST, IT WAS DARK.

Then Drew said, "Hey man, what's up?"

Logan wasn't startled—it was a sunny afternoon, and he'd felt Drew's shadow over him even before Drew had spoken. He opened his eyes and looked up. Drew's smile hovered about a million miles above him. Or so it seemed with Logan lying flat on his back and Drew standing at full height. From Logan's perspective on the grass, Drew looked like one of those comic book gods in the movies. Or at least a demigod: half human-half god, all buffed up and chiseled, and clad in nothing but his gym shorts. It was a warmer than average day for mid-October, though in Logan's reckoning not nearly warm enough to be running around shirtless—even for a guy whose last name happened to be Thor.

Logan gazed at Drew with a casual air of appraisal, but offered no comment on his scant attire; the guy could run about the pitch stark naked, for all Logan cared.

"So, is this where you spend your free period," Drew

asked with a clever smile, "catching rays on the soccer field?" He laughed—not a taunting laugh but a genuine one, the sort you'd share with a good friend. "Not a bad spot," he added, looking around the empty pitch.

"Nah," Logan said with a short yawn, "I just needed a quiet place to think."

"You picked a good one," Drew said, "except for eleven till noon. Coach likes to use the gym for extra practice time while he's got most of the team in the same class."

"I thought you were a swimmer," Logan said with mild indifference.

"I am," Drew said with a smile. "I also play soccer."

"Impressive."

Drew laughed. "Not if you've seen me play soccer."

"Maybe you should stay in the water."

Drew laughed again, though he wasn't altogether sure that Logan was joking.

From the far edge of the pitch, an adult voice called out: "THOR! ANY TIME TODAY WOULD BE NICE!"

Logan remained on his back with his hands behind his head, but he shot a surreptitious side glance at the touchline where Coach was going over a playbook with a group of boys who all looked like demigods in the making, though none quite as visually stunning as the mighty Drew Thor. A few of the boys glanced out at the pitch, then quickly turned their attention back to Coach, who held his stormy gaze on Logan before turning back to the playbook.

Logan's casual eye lingered on the touchline a moment longer. "I take it he's still pissed?"

Drew chuckled. "Oh yeah. Coach is like an elephant. He never forgets."

Though Drew had only just transferred here this year, the story of Logan's clash with Coach was legendary. Back in his sophomore year, Logan was in Coach's gym class and, as the story went, Coach had been so impressed with Logan's natural athletic ability that he asked him to join the soccer team on the spot. Of course, Coach, being Coach, didn't actually *ask* Logan anything. According to several boys who were there, before the final bell, Coach called out in his booming voice: "Kōtarō! You're on the team. Practice. Today. Four p.m. Sharp."

There had been no heads-up clash between the two of them when Logan didn't show up for practice, no heart to heart coach-player talk in the office adjacent to the locker room, no inspirational "movie moment" where the star player breaks his leg and the brooding loner who'd refused to join the team suddenly steps up to defend his school's honor, win the big game, and be hoisted onto the shoulders of his teammates while the coach who knew all along that he could do it smiles proudly from the sidelines. In fact, Coach never spoke directly to Logan after that day. Not even in gym class. If he needed to convey an instruction, he did it through one of the boys.

And today was no exception. The moment Coach spotted Logan lying out on the pitch, he boomed: "Thor! Go out there and wake His Royal Highness and get his brooding royal ass off my playing field before I have a royal frickin hemorrhage."

Of course, Drew didn't say this to Logan. He didn't have to; Coach's voice carried well, and by the ghost of a smile that played at one corner of Logan's mouth, Drew was pretty sure that Logan had heard Coach's demand loud and clear. Still, he made no attempt to move. He just lay there comfortably with his eyes closed, as if he hadn't a care in the world.

Despite his respect for Coach, Drew couldn't help feeling a twinge of respect for Logan as well. Regardless of what Coach thought, the guy was definitely not a poser, and he certainly wasn't about to acquiesce to anyone's demands—whether delivered directly or through an intermediary. Coach would have called this "active obtusity," but Drew knew better. Drew knew that Logan Kōtarō was anything but obtuse. In Drew's reckoning, Logan was like a locked door . . . and like all locked doors, all you needed to gain entry was the right key.

"I was a little surprised when you didn't call me."

Drew said this in a casual tone, as if just making small talk, but by the scarcely perceptible shift in Logan's peaceful expression, he could feel the key sliding into the lock, and now all he had to do was turn it.

"I was just curious how it went with the scene." He paused briefly before adding: "You said it was a three-part project, so I was just wondering when you were gonna call me to start working on the next part."

Logan lay perfectly still.

Drew laughed, though it came off more like a nervous chuckle. "Or did I suck so badly that you decided to recast my part?"

Logan remained still and silent. Drew waited before pressing on, a little faster than he'd intended.

"I'm not an actor, and I know that it's important to you, and I don't want you to get a shitty grade just because of me, so it's OK, you can tell me the truth. It's your project, and I won't be offended if you thought I sucked."

A long silence followed, in which Drew had more than enough time to question whether the key's notches had actually hit all the tumblers in the lock.

Then Logan spoke without opening his eyes. "You didn't suck."

With those words, the lock popped, and the door opened a crack. Without hesitation, Drew stuck his foot inside to prevent the door from slamming shut.

"Then we're still on for the other two scenes, I guess, right?"

Logan remained still and silent. Drew gently put his shoulder into the door, edging it open a little more.

"I'm losing my fear," he said with a small smile. "I think I need a refresher course. How about I come by your place tonight?"

He winced inside at his passive approach, but Logan's expression didn't change. He didn't say no to Drew's offer, but he looked as though he might be considering a response.

Drew was about to back off, give Logan a little space, when Coach's voice came booming from the touchline: "ANY DAY NOW, THOR!"

Whether it was the jolt of Coach's sudden interjection or something from within that told him to act quickly, Drew threw caution to the wind and shoved the door wide open.

"I've got to get back before Coach goes into an apoplectic fit," he said. "I'll see you at your place tonight."

Without waiting for a response, Drew turned and headed back toward Coach and the team. He didn't look over his shoulder along the way. He didn't need to. He knew that Logan would be gone by the time he reached the touchline.

As the players took the field, Drew felt a chill and

grabbed his shirt from the bench. He slipped it on and was heading out to join the others when Coach's voice halted him. It wasn't Coach's commanding tone, or even his irritated grumble; it came off more like a muttered side comment from someone who was otherwise preoccupied, which made sense because Coach was still scanning his playbook when he said it.

"Steer clear of that kid, Thor," Coach said as he flipped a page and squinted at the notes scribbled in the margin. "Trust me, when the egg finally cracks, you don't want the mess that's floating around in his screwy noggin leaking out onto you. That shit'll give you nightmares."

Drew wasn't sure how to respond, so he gave a half-smile the way he always did when he assumed Coach was being sarcastic. But when Coach looked up from the playbook, there was no hint of humor in his eyes.

It was half past six and already dark when Drew got out of his car and headed up the brick path to Logan's front door. He was about to ring the bell when he noticed a sheet of paper held in place between the ornate brass knocker and the strike plate. It was folded in half with his name written on the outside flap. The message inside was brief and cryptic:

COME IN. GO STRAIGHT DOWN THE HALL TO THE KITCHEN. FURTHER INSTRUCTIONS AWAIT THERE.

A sly smile curled at the corner of Drew's mouth. A little intrigue and mystery to start things off was cool by him. After all, he did come here to work on the second part of the scene they'd started last week. The first part had been loaded with intrigue and mystery—more than enough to pique his curiosity—and he was eager to find out what would come next.

The foyer was lit by the flickering flame of a jack-o'-lantern—an eerie light which cast huge shadows down the long front hallway. In the kitchen, a single dim light above the sink illuminated the spotless counters and appliances. There was a cozy breakfast nook nestled by a huge bay window, which overlooked the sprawling back lawn. Drew had never been in this part of the house before. When he'd come over to do the first part of the scene, Logan had led him straight up to his bedroom, so he'd only caught a glimpse of the showplace living room to the left of the foyer as he'd followed Logan upstairs.

There was another note waiting for him on the counter next to the sink.

It read:

YOU'VE COME THIS FAR, SO WE'LL ASSUME THAT YOU WISH TO CONTINUE. IF THIS IS AN INCORRECT ASSUMPTION, PLEASE DISREGARD THE REST OF THIS NOTE AND LEAVE NOW—THERE WILL BE NO HARD FEELINGS SHOULD YOU CHOOSE NOT TO STAY.

IF, HOWEVER, YOU DO WISH TO CONTINUE, THEN PLEASE CAREFULLY READ THE FOLLOWING INSTRUCTIONS.

IN THE GAMING ROOM DOWN THE FLIGHT OF

STAIRS OFF THE KITCHEN YOU WILL FIND YOUR GUIDE WAITING FOR YOU.

DO NOT DISTURB HIM. WAIT PATIENTLY WHILE HE FINISHES WHATEVER HE'S DOING. DO NOT ATTEMPT TO SPEAK TO HIM UNTIL HE INITIATES A DIALOGUE. WHEN HE DOES ENGAGE YOU, ADHERE STRICTLY TO THE FOLLOWING RULES:

1. LISTEN TO EVERYTHING HE HAS TO SAY BEFORE RESPONDING—DO NOT PRESUME TO INTERRUPT OR CONTRADICT HIM.

2. FOLLOW ANY AND ALL INSTRUCTIONS HE GIVES YOU, WITHOUT QUESTION.

3. DO NOT SPEAK HIS NAME, EVEN IF HE OFFERS IT. IF YOU FEEL IT ABSOLUTELY NECESSARY, YOU MAY ADDRESS HIM AS "L" (AS IN THE TWELFTH LETTER OF THE ALPHABET).

4. DO NOT PRESUME TO KNOW HIS MOTIVES OR WHAT HE'S THINKING. IF IN DOUBT, ASK. IF HE FINDS YOUR QUESTION VALID, HE WILL OFFER A REASONABLE EXPLANATION; IF NOT, HIS SILENCE ON THE MATTER IN QUESTION WILL SUFFICE.

5. REGARDLESS OF HIS ACTIONS OR WORDS, YOU WILL PROTECT AND DEFEND HIM—WITH YOUR LIFE, IF NECESSARY—AGAINST ANY AND ALL THREATS (UP TO AND INCLUDING ANY HARM

HE MIGHT POSE TO HIMSELF), AND YOU WILL DO SO WITHOUT BREAKING ANY OF THE FIRST FOUR RULES.

IF YOU FOLLOW THESE INSTRUCTIONS—EXPLICITLY AND WITHOUT DEVIATION—YOU WILL BE SAFELY DELIVERED TO YOUR ULTIMATE DESTINATION WHEN THE TIME IS RIGHT.

IF YOU FEEL THAT YOU CANNOT ABIDE BY THESE RULES, TURN BACK NOW AND LEAVE—AGAIN, THERE WILL BE NO HARD FEELINGS.

IF, HOWEVER, YOU CHOOSE TO GO ON AND AT ANY POINT FAIL TO ABIDE BY THE AFOREMENTIONED RULES, THE CONSEQUENCES WILL BE DIRE.

I AM ENTRUSTING YOU WITH THE LIGHT OF MY LIFE. DO NOT DISAPPOINT ME.

As Drew reread the last line of the note, a queer tingle ascended his spine. It was not an unpleasant sensation. Indeed, it felt distantly familiar, like the touch of a facile hand from a scarcely remembered dream. A cool caress that made him feel paradoxically warm.

He stood there at the counter while the clock on the wall behind him ticked away untold seconds and select lines from the note seemed to float off the page in smoky wisps . . .

. . . you've come this far . . . do not disturb him . . . do not

presume . . . do not speak his name . . . follow all instructions . . . if in doubt, ask . . . you may address him as "L" . . . defend him with your life . . .

Once again, the small smile curled at the corner of Drew's mouth, only this time it was more tentative than sly. He was still up for the second part of the scene—there was no way he could possibly resist such a blatant challenge, not after reading this note, which had all but begged him to turn and walk away with his tail between his legs. And yet he felt a sliver of apprehension—the same sort that had crept at the back of his mind when Logan had first approached him on that brisk afternoon in the student parking lot shortly after the final bell one week ago.

He had stepped up to the challenge then, without having any idea what lay ahead. But now, having completed the first part of the scene, he at least knew what to expect. He knew that Logan would be waiting for him in the gaming room downstairs. He knew that Logan would already be in character (the mysterious "L"). And he understood the "rules" of the scene . . . which he felt certain were specifically designed to get him to break character. He could see Logan (or "L") deliberately doing and saying things to get under his skin, just as he had done during the first part of the scene up in the bedroom—things that, much to Drew's embarrassment, had worked to varying degrees. The condescending tone of voice Logan had used, the glint of disdain in his eyes when he'd looked at Drew had seemed almost too real at times, as if Logan hadn't been acting at all. And Drew's responses had been very real. Logan *had* gotten under his skin.

But this time it would be different. This time, Drew would be going into the scene prepared. There would be no angry flare-ups, no telltale signs that Logan's cool stingers had hit their marks. He knew Logan's game, and he was prepared to show him that he was capable of playing more than just the "dumb jock."

He nodded confidently as he placed the note back on the counter. Then he took a measured breath and let it out slowly before heading to the stairs just off the kitchen.

The house was built on a slope, so the gaming room, which was technically located downstairs, opened onto the vast expanse of the well-manicured back garden, which was visible through the tall and wide glass wall on the north side of the spacious room. The gaming room itself was like something out of a kid's dream. A massive flat-screen television dominated the east wall, with two rows of plush leather recliners, the back row elevated so that the seats in front wouldn't block the screen. The west end of the room was devoted to arcade video games, pinball machines, and table games, all polished and gleaming beneath the ambient overhead lighting.

But despite all the luxurious accoutrements, Drew's eyes were immediately drawn to the center of the room, where a boy of no more than ten stood before a triad of models—the great pyramids, constructed solely of dominoes. At first, Drew didn't know which surprised him more: the unexpected boy or the magnificent domino structures, the largest of which stood nearly as tall as the boy himself.

Drew was speechless for a moment. Then he found his voice and said, "Hey, how's it going? I'm a friend of Logan's. Do you know where he—"

The boy cut him off: "Do you have an ocular deficiency? Or were you never taught to read properly?"

The boy's gaze remained fixed on the center pyramid,

as if Drew weren't even there—or worse, as if Drew were a servant who'd forgotten his place and broken etiquette by speaking out of turn.

Drew's cheeks burned at the casually blunt and disdainful tone of the boy's voice. It felt like he'd been slapped, and by a kid, no less. He was about to respond when something twinkled on his periphery.

It was a framed photograph on a shelf filled with framed photographs. It held a prominent place at the shelf's center, but that wasn't what made it stand out from the others. It was the *subjects* of this particular photograph that had caught Drew's eye: two boys whose resemblance was so striking they could have been twins, save for the age gap between them, which appeared to be five or six years. The older boy in the photo was clearly Logan; the younger was the boy who presently stood before the three pyramids of dominoes, with his silky dark hair overhanging his solemn grey eyes. Like Logan, the boy had a regal air about him, as if he stood a little taller with his raised chin and chiseled features, as if he belonged to a time when aristocracy reigned and proper table manners ranked higher than common courtesy . . . at least when interacting with commoners.

Commoners like me, Drew thought, and suddenly something clicked in his mind.

His gaze shifted from the photograph of the two boys (smiling boys in a happy place and time) to the intensely focused kid at the center of the gaming room, and the words written on the note in the kitchen upstairs suddenly came floating back to him . . .

. . . *do not disturb him . . . do not presume . . . follow all instructions . . . protect him . . . I am entrusting you with the light of my life . . .*

Drew stared at the boy as realization washed over him. Just when he'd thought he had Logan's game figured out, the smooth bastard had thrown him another curve. Having already done the first part of the scene with Logan—and knowing what to expect—Drew had felt fairly confident coming over here to play out the second part of the scene tonight. But in one cunningly brilliant move, Logan had shifted everything, forcing Drew to have to start from scratch—and with a brand new acting partner: Logan's steely-eyed look-alike kid brother. The mysterious "L."

Drew couldn't help smiling a small, rueful smile of admiration. Logan had trumped him again. No doubt about it.

But Drew wasn't about to give up that easily. He'd come here to do the scene, and he fully intended to see it through to the end. He stood at the foot of the stairs and patiently watched as the boy went about the methodical task of adjusting dominoes—some by mere fractions, others by more than an eighth of an inch. At one particularly precarious point, Drew held his breath, almost certain that the center pyramid would collapse. But the boy's small and steady hand made the correction without causing the slightest tremor in the structure.

As he continued to work on the pyramids, the boy said, "Do you know what makes it work, the domino factor?"

His tone was cool and casual. Sensing that the question was more rhetorical than practical, Drew waited for the boy to continue. And in time, he did.

"Precision," said the boy without breaking from his

task. "One carelessly placed tile will break the chain reaction and spoil the desired effect." He paused and then added, "Do you know what that is? Make an effort at a response, please."

Drew shrugged and said, "To make all the dominoes fall."

"No," the boy said evenly, his eyes still focused on his work. "Any fool can topple a row of tiles. Do I look like a fool to you? Make an effort at a *coherent* response, please."

The muscles in Drew's jaw tensed, and he said, "Why don't you just tell me what the desired effect is?"

The boy's cool grey eyes shone dark as he made the final adjustment—a single tile moved less than a fraction of an inch at the bottom of the center pyramid. Then he stood up straight and spoke with calm conviction: "It is the calculated destruction of perfection."

They stood there for a moment, the two of them, gazing at the pyramids in silence.

Then, without preamble, the boy tripped the starting block with the toe of his shoe, and the complex trail of dominoes that encircled the three pyramids began to fall in a perfect winding pattern, like a lit fuse rapidly burning its way to the bomb. At the back end, the chain suddenly broke off into three separate directions, each headed for its own pyramid.

The first to go was the smallest of the three. The point of impact occurred at the base, but the pyramid didn't simply collapse, as Drew had fully expected it would. Instead, it was as if an invisible force had chewed its way through the side of the pyramid and began devouring it from the inside out.

The evisceration of the other two pyramids followed in

rapid succession, and in less than sixty seconds, what must have taken hours—if not days, or even weeks—to construct, lay in a pile of rubble on the polished hardwood floor.

A brief silence followed, during which the boy's eyes looked almost mournful.

Drew waited a moment before saying, "Impressive."

The boy's gaze remained fixed on the rubble of his creation. "Yes, it was." Then he added, matter-of-factly: "I'm hungry. Did you drive here?"

The boy didn't wait for a response. He simply turned away from the pile of dominoes on the floor and headed upstairs. Drew followed.

When the boy saw Drew's Mustang in the driveway, he said, "I'm not riding in that."

Drew was struck again by the bluntly imperious tone, but he didn't take the bait. Instead, he shook his head lightly and said, "Well, it's that or nothing, little man."

The boy shot him a disdainful look, as if Drew had spoken in some vulgar foreign tongue. Then he reached into his pocket and produced a mobile device. In a swift series of smoothly executed thumb strokes, he activated the device's touch screen and punched in a four-digit code. Behind him, the three separate garage doors opened in unison. The stalls were double wide, each large enough to house two vehicles comfortably, though there were only four vehicles inside. Drew guessed that the two missing cars belonged to Logan's mother and sister, who both appeared to be out for the night. Of the four remaining vehicles, which included a Jaguar XJ, a Bentley Flying Spur, and a Mercedes GL350 SUV, Drew recognized only one—a black Porsche 911, which belonged to Logan.

Drew gazed at the Porsche for a moment. Then he

looked up to the darkened window of Logan's bedroom. He tried to picture Logan standing up there in the darkness, watching the scene unfold in the driveway below, but it didn't make sense. Was Logan really going to allow his kid brother to take off with Drew like this? How would he be able to monitor the progress of the scene? Was he just going to leave it to chance? That didn't seem like Logan at all.

Drew was still looking up at Logan's bedroom window when the boy said decisively, "We'll take the Mercedes."

They had dinner at a posh restaurant on the lakefront. Though the night breeze was crisp and most of the patrons were seated at tables inside, the boy chose a table on the east patio with a fine view of the lake. The menu was written entirely in French, but Drew did his best to give the impression that he wasn't completely lost. The boy didn't seem to notice, and in the end, it didn't matter. When the waiter came, the boy ordered for both of them.

The waiter greeted them in French and introduced himself as Olivier. Drew felt a twinge of mild surprise when the boy responded in French as if it were his native tongue. After he'd finished ordering, the boy made a comment that elicited a knowing smile from Olivier, who looked only a couple of years older than Drew. When Olivier returned with their beverages, a brief exchange ensued, again in French, followed by a smattering of laughter from Olivier and a polite smile from the boy. Though Drew had no idea what they were saying, he was pretty sure it had something to do with him, and his cheeks burned with a mixture of irritation and embarrassment. But, remembering the rules, he kept silent.

After Olivier headed back inside, the boy opened the dessert menu. Drew was still looking in the direction that Olivier had gone when the boy spoke without looking up from the menu. "He thinks you look like The Arrow on TV. Very handsome and muscular. Olivier likes handsome and muscular Americans. He wanted to know if you were seeing anyone. I told him that you were terminally straight and that his considerable talent in the art of seduction would be entirely wasted on you."

Drew didn't know what to say. The irritation he'd felt at the boy and the waiter sharing a private laugh at his expense evaporated, but the embarrassment only intensified. As the boy continued to peruse the dessert menu, his tone remained casual.

"If my assumption was incorrect, I apologize. Olivier is euro-model beautiful—if your taste happens to run in that direction—and I would be more than happy to translate a message from you, if you'd like. But then he *does* speak fluent English, and is well-versed in modern American slang, so you could always just tell him yourself." He paused briefly and acquired an expression that might have passed for mild amusement on a more animated face. "Or the two of you could go on pretending there's a language barrier, which might allow for some interesting developments along the way, depending on what sort of games you like to play."

Drew didn't know what to say.

The boy looked up from the menu and, without taking a beat, added, "I'm thinking of the Strawberries Briand for dessert. If you've never tried it, you should. It's delicious."

Drew still looked nonplussed; if the kid was trying to shock him, he was doing a good job of it. He thought about the things Logan had done and said during the first part of the scene, things to rattle and shock him—all part of the scene, which Drew had had no problem with. But to hear the same sort of dialogue coming from a ten-year-old kid was a bit unnerving, to say the least. It *had* to be dialogue, Drew assured himself. No kid would talk like this.

Under any other circumstances, Drew would have taken this kid back to the SUV, driven him straight home, and told him to tell his older brother that the show was over. But his curiosity had gotten the better of him. He wanted to get to the final part of the scene and see how it all tied together. He wanted to know how it all ended. And the only way he could *get* to the final part of the scene was by following through with this part of it.

After appetizers, the meal, and dessert (Strawberries Briand, which was indeed delicious), the boy set his fork on his plate and said softly, "Everything goes in threes."

Drew looked at the boy's mournful countenance and thought of the three meticulously constructed pyramids— all crumbling to the floor at the toppling of a single domino, and the whim of a preternaturally self-possessed child— and a sudden sadness touched his heart.

When the check came, Drew reached for his wallet, and the boy smiled as one might smile at a scarcely ambulatory toddler making his first attempt at a run.

"No need to break the bank," the boy said with casual aplomb. "I've got it."

He produced a credit card and set it on the tray with the check, and the waiter, the darkly handsome Olivier, smiled a small, almost secretive smile as he receded with the tray.

Sensing Drew's abashment, the boy said, "It's only

money, of which my family has more than enough to burn. No offense was intended."

"None was taken," Drew replied with what he hoped was a convincing casual smile.

The boy's solemn eyes seemed to twinkle by the dim light of the patio, but there was no guile in his tone when he said, "I could buy you anything you like. A new wardrobe—those shoes you're wearing have certainly seen better days. Or a new car to replace the antiquated one you've been driving. We could go to the dealership of your choice and do that right now, if you like."

Though the words came out as casually as if he were suggesting they stop off for an ice cream or a cup of coffee. There was no hint of guile in the boy's solemn eyes. But Drew wasn't about to give the desired reaction. Instead, he just smiled and shook his head.

"Nah, I'm good."

"I wasn't referring to you," the boy said in that same casually blunt tone. "I was referring to the state of your car, which is anything but good."

Drew shrugged off the comment, hoping the boy hadn't caught the flicker of tension in his eyes, and said, "It gets me around."

The boy nodded agreeably enough, and for a moment it looked as though he was going to let it drop. But then he took a different tack.

"I could buy Olivier for you," the boy said.

This time, there was no mistaking the tension in Drew's eyes. His lips parted, but before he could speak, the boy continued in that maddeningly dispassionate tone that belied his age.

"I could pay him to spend the night with you and do whatever you like. I could get you a suite at any hotel in the city. Or if you prefer, I could book you a flight to any place in the world. You could arrive in Paris in time for lunch tomorrow, and then spend the rest of the afternoon and evening with Olivier in any one of the Presidential suites at the Royal Monceau. Or, if you prefer it cozy, I could book you a Signature one-bedroom suite with a jacuzzi and a view—the sunset is breathtaking at this time of year. And the pool in the spa is heaven. I rather think you'd like it. Olivier is quite the swimmer."

Drew stared at the boy for a moment, speechless. Then he released a short, soundless laugh and shook his head. The kid was good, he had to admit that much. All in all, equal to his older brother in the art of cutting commentary, but with a far more jarring effect, because he was just a skinny little kid. Still, Drew refused to be sucked into the downward spiral of crossing verbal swords with a child.

"You are into water sports, I take it," the boy added.

Drew shook his head again. "I'm not gonna have this conversation with you."

"You're not 'gonna,' eh? And why is that?"

"I'm just not gonna."

"Not 'gonna' again," the boy said with a raised brow. "Then what are you *going to* do?"

"I don't know. According to the rules, that's up to you, little man."

"Then answer the question, you unmitigated rube. Why are you not 'gonna' have this conversation with me?"

"I'm—" Drew began forcefully, but then he pulled back and continued calmly. "I'm not *going to* have an adult conversation with you, because you're just a kid."

"And you're an adult?"

"I'm older than you."

"And that makes you an adult?"

"It makes me the responsible party."

"The responsible party? Do you really talk like that, or are you trying to impress me?"

"I don't know," Drew said with a bitterness that surprised him. "Do you really talk like Harry Potter, or are you trying to impress me?"

"I've only just moved here," the boy said. "Would you prefer that I mimic the monosyllabic grunt of the average American?"

"If you've only just moved here, shouldn't you have a Japanese accent?"

The boy was unfazed. "I reckon I would . . . had I come from Japan. But since I was born and raised in my mother's home borough of Cheltenham, Gloucestershire, and have never set foot in my father's native country, it would be rather odd for me to speak with a Japanese accent."

Drew's eyes narrowed. "Your brother doesn't have an accent."

"My brother?"

"Logan," Drew said.

The boy gave a curious half-smile. "He's lived here for five years, and in that time he has . . . adapted." The word came out as if it were something better spat than swallowed. The boy paused for a contemplative moment, and his eyes shone darkly when he said, "Have you any other insulting queries for me? If not, I would appreciate an answer to *my* question."

A dull pulse throbbed at Drew's temples as he stared at the boy in mild confusion.

The boy clarified it for him. "You said that you were the 'responsible party'—responsible for what?"

"For you."

"For me?"

"Yep."

"And how is that?"

"The note said that I had to look after you."

"The note said that you were to *protect* and *defend* me. It also said that you were to follow any and all instructions I give, without question."

The boy paused briefly, and his eyes shone darkly. Drew held his tongue and waited for the boy to continue.

"To elucidate: I am neither your responsibility nor your charge. I am your guide and master. And you are nothing more than my bodyguard. A strong arm, should the need for your considerable and obvious physical attributes arise. *I* am in control here. You would do well to remember that."

Under the extreme pressure of the boy's cool grey gaze, Drew looked away. But this was a mistake.

"Look at me when I'm speaking to you," the boy said with sudden force.

A quick muscle spasm flared in Drew's jaw, and his hands tightened into fists under the table, but he held his temper as he turned his gaze back to the boy.

"Let me make something patently clear," the boy said in a deadly serious tone. "You are never to turn away from me when I'm speaking to you." He paused to let the weight of his words sink in before continuing. "You may snarl. You may roll your eyes or smile that contemptuous smirk of yours, but you will never again avert your gaze when I'm speaking to you. Do you understand that?"

The boy stared at him with cold conviction, and this

time Drew did not avert his gaze. He looked directly into the boy's solemn eyes, searching for the dividing line between reality and performance. There was simply no way this kid could be for real. It was all just part of the scene. It had to be.

Drew nodded and said, "I understand."

"And?"

Drew thought about the last line of the note Logan had left for him on the kitchen counter: *I am entrusting you with the light of my life. Do not disappoint me.* He swallowed hard and said, "And it won't happen again."

The boy held Drew in his gaze for a moment longer. Then he looked off to the glowing lights in the distance, where the faint sound of screaming and laughter could be heard drifting from the grounds of the amusement park on the other side of the lake. Halloween wasn't for another two weeks, but throughout the month of October, the spirit of the season came alive at Terror Fest every Friday, Saturday, and Sunday.

The boy gazed at the distant orange lights that lined the rails of the colossal wooden roller coaster, whose tallest hill stood against the night sky like a beacon under the moon. By Halloween, that moon would be full, and spirits once contained in their earthly haunts would be released to roam free. But for now, the *replication* of terror would have to suffice for those seeking thrills and chills.

The boy was still gazing out at the arc of orange lights beneath the half moon when he posed a simple yet curious question. Drew wasn't sure if it was the question itself or the oddly serene tone of the boy's voice, but regardless, a tiny shiver crept up his spine when the boy said, "Do you frighten easily?"

It was half past seven when they arrived at the park. The main entrance was crowded, but the lines moved at a fairly swift tick, and before long, they were standing in front of the stone pond, where the towering tree-limbed animatronic Pumpkinhead figure rose to its full height to greet them.

Drew looked down at the boy at his side and saw something in those sharp grey eyes that he hadn't seen before. The spark of wonder and excitement brimming just beneath the surface—restrained yet alive and itching to escape, it was the look of a normal ten-year-old boy. Drew was taken by surprise when a sudden wave of emotion for the boy washed over him. Drew had an older brother but no younger siblings. Though he and his brother got along very well, Drew had always secretly wished he'd had a younger brother, someone closer to his own age that he could hang out with and mentor. He'd had friends back in California, where he grew up, who blew off their kid brothers all the time, and though he'd never said a word about it to any of them, it had bothered him.

Looking down at Logan's kid brother now, Drew couldn't help wondering what their relationship was like. He imagined the two of them sitting across a table from one another, a chessboard between them, each taking turns until the last move was made and the loser laid down his king in defeat. A silent game between two calculative boys. No laughter, no small talk, no arguing over whose turn it was. Just cool precision and decisive moves.

It was a sad image that caused Drew's heart to swell painfully, and for a moment, he felt the urge to put his hand on the boy's skinny shoulder and give a reassuring squeeze, or to ruffle the kid's shiny dark hair with a brotherly wink and grin. The urge passed when the boy said, "Come," in a commanding tone and, without waiting, headed off toward The Screaming Demon, a winding and low-crawling steel coaster, which paradoxically had the steepest drop of any ride in the park.

The night didn't go quite as Drew had expected— though, in truth, he hadn't really known what to expect. The boy he'd met in the gaming room back at the house— the boy who'd watched the destruction of the magnificent triad of pyramids with ethereal composure, the boy who'd ordered dinner in French and casually spoke of soliciting the waiter for a night of debauchery, the boy who'd pierced Drew with that implacable grey gaze and told him in no uncertain terms just who was in charge—that boy began to recede.

It wasn't a magical transformation, and it didn't occur all at once. It came in gradual increments, with each layer of the hardened façade being chipped away, as if by a gentle hand with a fine chisel. The boy led the way, but each time he called out which ride they would be getting on next, his tone sounded less commanding. And though his countenance remained solemn, even on the most extreme rides, his eyes shone with genuine delight and excitement.

At one point, the boy surprised Drew by taking his hand. It happened in the dark tunnel leading up to The Drop Zone, which had been renamed "The Hell-e-vator" for Halloween. It had surprised Drew not only because it was an uncharacteristic gesture for such a self-possessed kid but also because the boy had shown no fear whatsoever on the haunted walk through Necropolis, where eerie music and sound effects rose from hidden speakers along the path, and every imaginable monster lurked in the shadows, waiting to pop up and scare the living daylights out of passersby. Even when they'd reached the entrance to the big covered bridge at the end of the haunted walk (a juncture at which most opted for the little detour path that led back into the main park), the boy had headed straight for the bridge with fearless determination. And despite the grinding buzz of a chainsaw that emanated from the surrounding darkness, the boy had paused halfway through to watch the masked maniac chase a group of screaming teenagers around.

But inside the tunnel leading up to The Hell-e-vator, a free-fall ride with a two-hundred-and-twenty-seven-foot drop, the boy had quietly taken Drew's hand and moved a little closer to him. Drew's heart swelled at this display of vulnerability and trust, and suddenly, he felt protective of the boy. Suddenly, he felt the urge to kneel down and look the boy in the eye and tell him that it was all right to be afraid, that there was nothing to be ashamed of. He wanted to tell him that he didn't have to get on the ride if he didn't want to. They could leave the line and go wherever the boy liked. But he knew he couldn't do that. The boy was determined to prove that he was not afraid of anything. Drew could see the resolve emanating from those cool grey eyes, focused and fixed on the towering spire of the ride, even as the boy's grip on his hand grew tighter.

When they reached the end of the tunnel and the gates opened to let the next group of riders on, the boy released Drew's hand and headed straight for the open seat on the end. He hopped up into the seat and buckled in, but before he could bring the padded steel harness down over his shoulders, Drew reached in to make sure that the straps were secure and snug.

"Are you apprehensive?" the boy said in a steady voice.

Drew smiled with uncertainty and said, "A little."

In truth, Drew did not like heights. He wasn't irrationally fearful of them; he just preferred to be on solid ground. He'd half expected the boy to make a comment after his confession, but the boy simply nodded. Drew brought the steel harness down over the boy's shoulders and tugged on it hard to make sure that it was locked in place before getting into his own seat and strapping in.

They sat with their legs dangling free while the attendants came around to make sure that everyone was securely locked in. Then the voice of the ride's operator came through the speakers in a spooky-sweet tone, wishing one and all a pleasant ride on The Hell-e-vator. He stretched out the last word with a delightfully creepy chuckle before pressing the button to start the ride.

As the ride began its long ascent, Drew caught sight of something at the tunnel's opening. Tucked into the misty shadows, there stood three boys, all lined up perfectly, side by side, from the shortest to the tallest.

This in itself wasn't odd. What *was* odd was that the three boys were all dressed in identical attire: steel-toed leather shoes, black trousers, and long-sleeved black T-shirts with strategic tears. Their bodies were lean yet chiseled, their faces painted harlequin white. All three gazed up at the ascending ride with shining silver eyes. It was an eerie sight that gave Drew a chill. But even more eerie was that, save for the difference in their heights and ages, they could have been identical triplets.

The three boys disappeared from view when the ride

hit the quarter mark trigger and sped rapidly to the top, where it locked into place with an abrupt metallic clanging sound. Drew closed his eyes, but the image of those boys staring out from the tunnel still hovered in his mind.

For a moment, all was silent, and the only thing Drew could hear was the intermittent sound of the flags flapping on the towering pole in the distance.

Then the boy, L, spoke to him.

"They're not real," he said, his soft voice cutting calmly through the whipping wind. "He wants you to see them so that you'll be afraid. Don't give in to your fear. Open your eyes, and they'll go away."

Drew held his eyes shut for a moment longer, and when he finally opened them, the image of the three boys vanished. It was replaced by a stunning view of the crisp night sky over the highway that stretched out to the north of the park and well beyond. And though the cold wind stung his eyes, he did not close them. Not even when the lock released and the suspended seats went plunging straight downward at breakneck speed.

When the harnesses unlocked and they were safely back on the ground, Drew looked to the opening of the tunnel, expecting to see the three boys emerge to take their seats on the ride, but they weren't among the next group of riders. They had simply disappeared.

Drew was still looking toward the tunnel when the boy announced that he was thirsty and headed off for the nearest snack station. He bought two cups of steaming hot chocolate and gave one to Drew. They strolled around the park for a while, quietly sipping their drinks and observing the festivities. Drew thought about asking the boy to elaborate on what he'd said when they were at the top of The

Hell-e-vator waiting for the drop, but suddenly he wasn't so sure that he'd heard the boy speak at all. With the howling wind and flapping flags, perhaps he'd only imagined that he'd heard the boy speaking. Or maybe the boy had spoken, and Drew had merely misunderstood what was said. It was possible.

But still, he couldn't have imagined those three boys looking out from the tunnel with their shining silver eyes.

They're not real. He wants you to see them so that you'll be afraid. Don't give in to your fear. Open your eyes, and they'll go away.

And they had gone away. All three of them. Gone by the time the ride had returned safely to the ground.

Everything goes in threes.

The boy had said that back at the lakefront, after the dessert dishes had been cleared away, and in Drew's mind now, three things flashed by: the three course dinner at the bistro, the destruction of the three pyramids of dominoes back at the house, and the three boys staring out from the tunnel at the ride. As these images collided in a subtle explosion, another tiny chill crept up Drew's spine. The sensation doubled when the memory of something Logan had said up in the bedroom last Friday came flooding back into Drew's consciousness . . .

. . . everything goes in threes . . . this is only the beginning . . . there are still two more acts to come . . .

Drew was still lost in thought when he realized that the boy had stopped at the edge of a crowd gathered around a bandstand, where a group of zombies was jamming on electric guitars while the wolf-man rocked out on the drums. The half shell background was lit with colored lights and strobes, which made the performers appear to move in eerie slow motion. They had just finished a rousing version of Lifehouse's *Just Another Name*, and while the crowd was still cheering, they rolled into a fairly impressive rendition of Queen's *Bohemian Rhapsody*.

As the boy watched the zombie band with intense focus, Drew felt another wave of compassion for him. When the boy's eyes filled with emotion at the tragic final line of the song, a sad smile touched Drew's lips, and once again he felt the urge to put his hand on the boy's shoulder and give a reassuring squeeze. But, as before, he resisted the urge. The boy had more pride than Drew had ever seen in any kid his age, and Drew didn't want to risk wounding that pride—certainly not after the boy had offered the small but significant gesture of trust by taking his hand in the darkened tunnel back at the Hell-e-vator.

The tenderness that had appeared in the boy's eyes during the *Bohemian Rhapsody* vanished on the opening bars of the next number: The Cure's *Three Imaginary Boys*. The rhythmic strumming of the guitars, along with the driving beat of the drums, sent a wave of gooseflesh over Drew's arms. But the boy simply turned and walked away with a composed expression that belied the frosty glint in his eyes.

They headed toward Blood River, but the rafts weren't running, so they cut across the path to the larger of the park's two wooden roller coasters, a sprawling out-and-back called The Spirit. It was a classic ride with huge hills and a top speed of 70 mph, but for Drew's money, the coiling maze of The Silver Bullet, which was loaded with countless twists and turns and plenty of air time, had the larger coaster beat hands down. Drew assumed the boy shared his opinion and was saving the smaller wooden coaster for the last ride of the night. And he was correct. It was the boy's favorite and indeed his intended final destination. But something happened in the queue leading up to The Spirit—an unexpected twist that changed everything, and the course of the night's events shifted into a decidedly darker direction.

The queue was extra long and moved more slowly than usual because only one of the two side-by-side trains was running tonight. They were in the thick of the crowd on the long steel bridge above the south driveway when Drew noticed a couple of girls smiling at him. One was short with chestnut hair and light brown eyes that sparkled when she smiled; the other was a strawberry blonde with eyes that seemed to shift from blue to green depending on the way the light hit them. Both were very pretty and looked familiar, but he was fairly certain they didn't go to his school.

When the shorter girl called out the name of their school, Drew nodded with a smile of recognition. He'd seen them at the swim meet in New Lennox a couple of weeks ago. He'd assumed they were there to support the home team, but when he'd smoked New Lennox's top guy in the last leg of the 400 medley, they'd both stood and cheered for him. After the meet, they'd introduced themselves (though, for the life of him, Drew could not remember either of their names), and the short one with the chestnut hair and dazzling eyes had given him her number and made him promise to call her.

He never did call—he wasn't even sure what had happened to the scrap of paper with her number on it—and looking at her now, Drew couldn't help feeling a little guilty. But the girl didn't seem upset in the slightest. In fact, she was smiling as she and her friend cut backwards in the queue to join him.

They chatted all the way up to the ride. The shorter girl did most of the chatting, while Drew smiled and nodded, and the strawberry blonde laughed with embarrassment every time her friend said something to make Drew blush. Drew didn't really mind, though. He understood that it was just harmless flirting, and he actually enjoyed their company. The only awkward moment came when the shorter girl gave Drew a shrewd but not unkind smile and said, "You don't remember our names, do you?"

Drew's cheeks flushed, but the taller girl came to the rescue by shrieking her friend's name in admonishment, "*Danae!*"

The shorter girl laughed and said, "Good one, Marilyn, just feed him the answers while I've got him on the ropes here!" She immediately chuckled at her own mistake of giving up Marilyn's name, which, of course, wasn't really a mistake at all, and then, still smiling, she turned to Drew and said, "Tell the truth, and I'll believe you, did you really remember our names?"

Drew smiled innocently and said, "Sure, you're Danae, and she's Marilyn," and that got all of them cracking up.

They were almost at the top of the hill when the shorter girl, Danae, asked which one of them Drew would like to sit next to on the ride. She was smiling coyly, and her tone was teasing, but Drew could see in her eyes that at least a small part of her was serious. Before he could answer, Danae suggested that he take the first ride with Marilyn, and when they got back, he could take another ride with her.

"*If* you're not too scared to get back on again," Danae added with a chuckle and a delightful shiver. "I know that *I'll* feel a lot safer with those big, strong arms around me."

Drew couldn't help laughing. The girl was sweet and funny, and he genuinely liked her.

Danae read his hesitation even before he started to shake his head, and with a playfully shrewd eye, she said, "Hey, you're not gonna try to back out on us here, are you?"

"Nah," Drew said, "it's just that I'm here with—" He stopped short and looked to his side, but the boy was no longer there. He looked around quickly, certain that he would spot him, but the boy was nowhere in sight.

Suddenly, his blood ran cold. He'd thought this was something that only happened in books, like when the narrator announces dramatically, "His blood ran cold," but to Drew's surprise, it was actually true: his blood literally had gone cold. As he scanned the queue behind them, real panic began to creep in.

At first, Danae thought he was joking and was ready to call him on it, but Marilyn put a hand on her arm to keep her quiet. When Drew started asking people if they'd seen a ten-year-old boy, and if anybody had seen where he went, Danae's smile was replaced by a look of grave concern.

"Are you talking about that kid with the dark hair and spooky intense eyes?" Danae said. It was the wrong way to put it, and she immediately got a pained expression at her verbal blunder, but Drew was only concerned with what she might have seen.

"Did you see which way he went?"

"No. I mean, I saw him, but I thought he was with those people behind us. Is he your little brother?"

Drew was scanning the area beyond the queue now,

the dark expanse of the park, which seemed to stretch out like an infinite landscape from some scary movie, or a nightmare—one from which there was no escape.

Drew called out, "L!" But no response came back.

"Look," Danae said, "I'm sure he's all right. He probably just— Jesus, you're trembling."

She took hold of Drew's hand, and he shivered at her touch.

"He couldn't have gone far," Danae said. "I just saw him like thirty seconds ago, I think. He probably had to use the bathroom. Or maybe he saw something that grabbed his interest on the way here and just went back to see it. Kids are always doing things like that. They get something in those little heads of theirs, and they can't get it out, you know? I mean, am I right?"

Danae looked at Marilyn to back her up, and Marilyn chimed in, "Oh yeah."

"You see?" Danae said with a bright smile that did little to allay the fearful look in her eyes. "He's fine. We'll just retrace your steps until we find him. And then we can *all* get on this crazy ride, or whatever ride the little guy likes."

Drew got a grip on himself and nodded. But in his mind, he could see the sheet of paper on the kitchen counter. The note that Logan had left for him with the list of rules. In particular, the final rule: *Regardless of his actions or words, you will protect and defend him—with your life, if necessary—against any and all threats (up to and including any harm he might pose to himself).* And once again, the final line of the note rose in his mind's eye: *I am entrusting you with the light of my life. Do not disappoint me.* Only here and now, those words seemed to convey a far more ominous sentiment.

Danae and Marilyn were still looking at him with concern. Though he appreciated their concern and would have liked nothing more than to accept their offer to help find the boy, something told him that he would do well to handle this on his own. Drew had never been very good at lying, but he gave it a shot now and hoped it would be convincing.

He told Danae that she was probably right about L seeing something that had grabbed his interest along the way. He said he had a pretty good idea where the boy had gone off to and that it would be best if he went to get him on his own. He added with a guilty expression that he hadn't been the best older brother lately and that tonight was supposed to be a make-up for lost time, a "guys only" thing. He was ashamed at how easily the lies rolled off his tongue, but the shame only helped the lies seem all the more convincing; he actually looked like a guy drowning in guilt.

Danae squeezed his hand with a guilty look of her own. Her hand was cold, but her grip was compassionate and reassuring. Drew could see in her eyes that she felt miserable at the thought that she and Marilyn had intruded and possibly caused the boy to run off, and he assured her that it wasn't her fault, that it was his fault for turning his back on the boy. He shook his head, once again amazed at the ease with which the lies continued to flow.

But that last part wasn't really a lie, he thought, ruefully. *If I hadn't turned my back on the kid, none of this would be happening right now.*

He thanked the girls again for their concern, and as he turned to leave the queue, Danae asked if he still had her number. He stopped and shook his head—he'd told enough lies for one night.

"Give me your phone," Danae said. Drew handed it over. Danae went to his contacts list and added her name and number. "There. Now you have it for good. Just send us a text when you find him, so we won't be up half the night worrying ourselves sick."

Drew nodded and headed back into the park.

Following Danae's advice, he retraced his and L's steps, from the south end, where The Spirit was located, to Blood River, and all the way back to the haunted walk of Necropolis, where the buzz of the chainsaw still cut through the night like a horrifying siren. But there was no sign of the boy anywhere along the way.

After making a complete round of the park, Drew's panic reached a new level. He was no longer afraid of what Logan might do or say to him—he was long past worrying about his own hide. His only concern was for the boy. Though he talked a good game and seemed like a tough little kid, he was still just a kid, and Drew couldn't suppress the image of the boy huddled up in some dark corner of the park, alone and frightened, yet at the same time too stubbornly proud to come out of hiding.

Hoping that maybe the boy had just found a place to hide out near The Spirit, Drew headed back toward the south end of the park. He was nearly there when his phone started to buzz. As he fished it out of his pocket, he felt a sudden rush of hope: Danae and her friend Marilyn had found L and were calling to let him know where to meet them. He so desperately wanted this to be true that without even looking at his phone's screen, he pressed ANSWER and said breathlessly, "Please tell me that you found him?"

But the voice on the other end of the line was not Danae's. It was a familiar voice with a slightly silky tone and a decidedly cool edge, one that sent chilly tendrils racing over Drew's entire body. At first, he could have sworn it was Logan, calling to ask how the scene was going. But the voice was that of a child. It was the boy, L.

"I'm sorry to disappoint you, Drew," L said, "but your little girlfriends haven't been any more successful than you have at finding me. Though not for lack of effort—they're searching Blood River as we speak. Tenacious little tarts, those two. They must really be into your lugubrious protective older brother act. Lovely girls. Tell me, on the whole, which do you fancy more, the Elvish one with the eyes that change color, or the cute Hobbit with the shiny chestnut hair? She's no taller than I, that one. But she's got pluck, and her eyes are dazzling. Do you imagine they might both entertain you at once? One up top and the other down below? Is that the sort of thing that appeals to a bloke like you?"

The line went silent. Drew was speechless.

"Answer me, you pathetic toad," the boy commanded.

Drew swallowed hard and said, "Where are you?"

"Wouldn't you like to know," the boy replied, as if he believed anything but. "You have your harlots—they're headed toward the haunted walk now; if you pull a jerk, you can catch up to them and have a lovely evening. I can give you Olivier's mobile number, if you'd care to make your threesome a foursome—he swings both ways, you know—"

"Stop it," Drew said with sudden force. "Tell me where you are."

The line went silent again, and for a moment Drew thought the boy might have hung up on him.

Then the boy's voice came through with cool conviction:

"You really are thick, aren't you. After all that has gone before, you still don't get how this works, so allow me to clarify the rules. *I'm* the one who gives the orders. *You're* the one who obeys. You're nothing more than a toy that I deign to play with, and when I tire of you, you'll be discarded like any other object that has outlived its usefulness. Do you understand this? Or do you require further elucidation?"

Drew stood frozen as the cool night breeze washed over his face, but it did nothing to alleviate the fire that burned in his cheeks. His anger grappled briefly with his fear, but in the end, his fear won out, and he asked the boy again where he was. He told him that he would come get him and that they could do whatever the boy liked.

The line was silent again.

Then the boy said, "Do you think you can bargain your way out of this? Do you think that if you offer me an ice cream and a ride on the carousel, all will be forgiven? Do you think that just because you're bigger and stronger, I'll get frightened and come running to you for protection? Do you think I'm the sort who frightens easily? A weak little kid, lost in the dark? *Answer me, toad.*"

Drew's gut clenched, but he held it tight and said, "No. I don't think you're weak, and I don't think you're afraid."

Another moment of silence, longer this time.

Then the boy spoke again. "Are *you* afraid?"

Drew's heart pounded in a slow, driving throb, sending wave upon wave of blood crashing at his temples. "Yes," he said, his voice sounding distant to his own ears, "I'm afraid."

The boy took a measured pause before responding. "No, you're not," he said flatly. "Not yet, anyway. But you will be."

The line went dead, and once again Drew thought the boy had hung up on him. But the boy was still there on the other end. Drew couldn't hear him, but he could feel him. And there was something else. A faint sound in the background. Like pressurized air being released in a single thrust. A familiar sound, like an old steam train coming to a stop in the station.

Drew was listening hard to pick up on any other background noises when the boy's voice cut through the silence like a blade: "This is going to be a night you'll remember for the rest of your life. And every time you close your eyes, you'll see what your actions have wrought. Even if you don't get here in time to see it, the image will haunt your every dream, and you'll wake in the dead of night, drenched in sweat and screaming my name because you'll know that it was all your fault. You made this happen. *You* did this, and you have no one to blame but yourself."

The line went dead again, and this time it was clear that the boy had hung up. But not before Drew had heard one last sound coming from the background—a voice filtered through a tinny speaker: *"Thank you for challenging The Silver Bullet! We hope you enjoy the rest of your visit at Five Falls Terror Fest!"*

Drew didn't hesitate. He bolted across the park, faster than he'd ever run in his entire life. When he reached the huge sign that read Southwest Scare-i-tory, he bypassed The Silver Bullet's entrance queue and went straight for the exit. He weaved through the oncoming crowd of riders exiting The Bullet and raced along the narrow winding pathway to get to the house at the top of the hill, where the next group of riders was being loaded onto one of the two five-car trains. In his mind, he could see the boy, L, getting into one of the cars and bringing down the lap bar. He could see the boy leaving enough space between the bar and his lap for a nice airtime lift. He could also see how easy it would be for a kid the size of L to slip his skinny frame *out* of that loose lap bar once the ride was off and running. It was a terrifying thought, one that instantly chilled the sheen of sweat that had broken out over Drew's body.

Even if you don't get here in time to see it, the image will haunt your every dream, and you'll wake in the dead of night, drenched in sweat and screaming my name . . .

The steep flight of wooden steps leading up to the ride came into view, but just as Drew began to make the final dash, he spotted something within the coiling structure of The Silver Bullet. A faint glimpse of a moving shadow that he would have missed had he not turned his head at precisely the right moment. It was the silhouette of a small figure climbing the maintenance stairs that led up to the tracks at the center of the ride.

A cold hand gripped Drew's heart, and for a moment, he was frozen. Then his paralysis broke, and in a single bound, he jumped the fence of the exit queue and raced into the underbelly of The Bullet.

He reached the maintenance stairs quickly, but access was blocked by a tall wooden enclosure, whose gate was secured with a padlock. Along the north side of the enclosure, there was a loose board, through which the boy had gained easy entry, but the gap it created was not nearly wide enough for Drew to slip through. He didn't try to find another way in; there wasn't enough time. He raised his foot and started kicking at the locked gate. When it refused to give, Drew quickly shifted his energy to the loose board.

It only took a few steady yanks to break free, and the next plank, though more securely nailed down, came loose when Drew put all of his strength into it. The sound of the nails screeching in protest grated in his ears, but he continued to tug at the board with all his might, and within moments it was hanging loose, and he was able to slip through the opening with relative ease.

Drew took the stairs two at a time and reached the second platform in a flash, but the boy had a good head start on him and was already at the top, where the highest platform let out onto the tracks. Drew could hear the first train of cars in the distance, whizzing around the huge curve at the south end of the ride, and from there into the winding maze of the inner tracks. As the train approached the spot at the top of the maintenance stairs, the structure began to rumble. Then a brilliant series of flashes went off like a strobe light, illuminating the boy on the highest platform as the train whizzed by on the stretch of track behind him.

It was a stunning sight, both horrifying and electrifying at once. And just for a second, Drew could have sworn that he saw the three ethereal-looking boys from the tunnel of The Hell-e-vator's queue standing up there, their pale faces lit by the freakish flashing of those lights. But then, as the train sped off and the lights went out, all he could see was the boy, L, standing alone, his small hands on the rail, his silky dark hair fluttering in the powerful gust of wind.

For a split second, Drew felt frozen in time, unable to move or even think. He snapped out of his stupor when a new sound rose in the distance—a sound that sent a fresh wave of goosebumps racing over his body. The distinctive clickety-clack of the second train climbing the steep hill at the opposite end of the ride. And with that sound echoing in his ears, he raced the rest of the way up the wooden stairs. But just as Drew reached the highest platform, the boy backed up, ducked under the wooden safety rail behind him, and stepped out onto the tracks.

Drew's first instinct was to rush to the rail and reach out to pull the boy back to safety. But he fought the urge and instead extended a hand, palm open, in a calming gesture. The boy stood steady on the tracks, his grey gaze fixed intently on Drew, his skinny chest rising and falling with each measured breath, his dark hair swaying in the breeze. He looked both helpless and powerful, like a prince who has ascended to the throne only to discover that his kingdom has fallen and that his once-grand army has been cut down to a single loyal knight.

Me, Drew thought with sudden clarity as he gazed into the steel grey waters of the boy's eyes. *Right now, I'm all he's got. No one else is coming to save him—they'd never make it in time.*

With that thought, another wave of chilly tendrils raced Drew's spine, while somewhere in the distance the zombie band struck the first haunting chords of Exitmusic's *The Cold.* As the mournful ballad drifted into the night air and encircled the crisscrossing rafters of The Silver Bullet in an eerie embrace, the boy's eyes suddenly glistened with unspilt tears, and his voice rose like that of a newly crowned king, ready to charge headlong into the opposing army with no shield or weapon, other than his fragile heart and his unshakable pride.

"You swore an oath to me!" the boy shouted above the

combined sounds of the music, the wind, and the rumbling train, which had just crested the tall hill and plunged down the first steep drop. Then his words came tumbling out in a ferocious, unbroken stream. *"You swore that you would obey me and do everything I say! You read the rules and agreed to them! You could have backed out, but you chose to go forward! This was to be my night! My night! You broke the rules! And now you have to pay! I gave you this one chance, and you couldn't just take it! You thought you could cheat and get away with it, but not this time! Not this time! Go be with your girlfriends! Let them take you to the candleroom! That's what you want, and they know it! Go with them! I don't care! Let them push the button as many times as they like! They won't stop when you get dizzy! You'll see! You'll be the one! And I won't save you this time! I'll watch with the other boys, but I won't save you this time! I don't need you! I don't need anyone! I'm alone here! I'm the only one left! You're not here! You're not real! None of this is real! I hate you!"*

A single tear escaped and rolled down the boy's cheek, and Drew's heart tightened painfully. He hadn't understood everything the boy had said, but the main message had come through loud and clear. He had turned away from the boy to talk with the girls, and though he hadn't meant any harm, the result was the same.

He looked deeply into the boy's eyes now and saw the truth. Beneath all the bravado and tough talk, L was just a vulnerable little kid who wanted someone to make him feel like he mattered. Drew thought of Logan, the kid's real older brother. He thought of the scenes that Logan enjoyed constructing and setting into motion like complex configurations of dominoes, all toppling in perfect succession at his command. He thought of how Logan had used his kid brother tonight to continue the scene, and it brought an angry lump to his throat. One which he swallowed back because there wasn't any time to be angry at Logan right now. He needed to act fast, before the train made it to this section of the track. He needed to say something that the boy would not be expecting. Something that would jolt the kid back into reality because, contrary to what the kid had said about none of this being real, it was *very* real, and in less than sixty seconds, it was going to get even more real.

"You're right," Drew said, forcing himself to speak calmly. "I screwed up. I promised that it would just be you and me, and that we'd do whatever you wanted, and I broke that promise." He took a short breath, and with it, a calculated risk. "But I am not your older brother. And I'm not going to pretend that I have any power over you. I can't tell you what to do, and I don't want to."

The boy was eying him now, like a curious cat that wants to believe the extended hand will soothe and not strike.

Drew took another short breath and continued without taking his eyes off of L's. "What I can be is your friend . . . if you'll let me. And I can promise you that I will never turn my back on you again. I promise you that. If you ever need me, I'll be there. No matter where I am, no matter what I'm doing, you call me, and I'll be there. I can make you that solemn promise right here and now. And I won't screw up again."

The boy was trembling now, but he continued to hold back the tears stoically. He looked so tiny and helpless standing on the track that Drew had to fight the urge to lunge forward and scoop him into a protective embrace.

Instead, Drew looked deeply into the boy's eyes and took one last breath before nailing it home.

"Look at me and tell me if you believe I'm lying," he said. "If not, give me your hand."

The boy did not extend his hand, but Drew could see in his eyes that he was *thinking* about it, working it out like an equation beyond his comprehension, grappling with the desire to trust and the ingrained belief that all promises, including those most sincere, are eventually broken.

As the structure began to vibrate with the motion of the oncoming train, Drew worked to keep his desperation in check. "You asked me before if I was scared," Drew said in a shaky voice. "I'm not going to lie to you. I'm scared right now. More than I've ever been in my life." Drew held up his trembling hands to show the boy that he was indeed scared. "But I know that you're not. I know you're braver than I could ever be. And I need you to be brave enough for the both of us right now, OK? I need you to reach out to me because I'm not gonna be able to do this without you . . . "

The train was close now, very close. As it whizzed through the last few curves leading into the stretch of the track where L stood, the structure began to vibrate with such tremendous force that Drew was certain the boy would lose his balance and fall. But the boy didn't fall. Somehow, he kept his balance as he gazed into Drew's eyes, wanting to believe, wanting to take the leap and trust that Drew would be there to catch him.

As the train banked the final corner leading into the stretch of the track adjacent to the maintenance stairwell, it took every ounce of Drew's resolve to hold his tongue and not yell at the kid to take his hand right now. Instead, he offered the boy the only thing he could: his *own* trust. His absolute confidence in the boy—his blind faith that when he reached out over the rail, the boy would reach back and take his hand.

It happened in a split-second, like something out of a dream—one in which, no matter how hard you try, you simply cannot move fast enough to escape impending doom. One moment, the boy was on the track with the lead car of the train coming right at him; the next, he was on the platform, wrapped in Drew's embrace, as the train barrelled by in a frightening protracted blur. In its wake, the structure trembled fiercely, and Drew held the boy tightly, shielding his tiny frame with his own body until the platform became stable once again.

The boy's face was still buried against Drew's chest when the sound of the train pulling to a stop in the house beyond the final sweeping curve came drifting through the crossbeams of the structure like a gentle whisper, as if to acknowledge that the danger had passed and everything was now OK. But as Drew echoed this sentiment in a soothing tone, the boy continued to cling to him, as if he believed anything but. And as the pulsating wave of blood crashing at his temples subsided, Drew began to think the boy was right.

Everything was not OK.

In fact, things were about as far from OK as they could possibly get.

They got back to the house shortly after ten. The garage door was open. Drew pulled the Mercedes into its slot, killed the engine, and looked into the rearview mirror. The boy was sound asleep in the back seat. He did not wake, even when Drew opened the door and scooped him up into his arms; he simply curled up close with his head resting on Drew's shoulder and continued to breathe softly as Drew carried him to the front porch. The door was locked, but Drew found the house key on the ring next to the car key and let himself in.

He carried the boy up the long, curving staircase and only hesitated for a moment at the top. Logan's room was at the far end of the hall. No light came from underneath the door, but Drew could almost sense that someone was in there, waiting.

His jaw tensed at the thought of Logan sitting there in the dark, patiently waiting to hear how "the scene" had gone. Drew had no intention of speaking to Logan tonight, not after all that had happened at the amusement park. His only concern now was for the boy. He would get him tucked into bed and then wait downstairs for Logan's mother or sister to come home. In his mind, he could hear Coach's warning from earlier today on the touchline of the soccer pitch . . .

Steer clear of that kid, Thor. Trust me, when the egg finally cracks, you don't want the mess that's floating around in his screwy noggin leaking out onto you. That shit'll give you nightmares.

. . . and he was not about to leave the boy alone in the house with Logan.

There was a night light burning from an open door just down the hall, and when Drew looked inside, he knew at once that this was L's bedroom. It was a kid's dream room, elaborately designed and decorated to look like a cozy Hobbit-hole from *The Lord of the Rings* movies.

The boy stirred and clung closer when Drew took him to the bed and pulled back the covers. Drew gently rubbed the boy's small back, and when the boy relaxed his grip, Drew set him on the bed and carefully removed his jacket and shoes. He found a fresh pair of pyjamas in the top drawer of the wardrobe and managed to get the boy out of his clothes and into the pyjamas without waking him, at least not fully. The boy opened his eyes a few times, but the razor-sharp alertness that had been there before was replaced by the dreamy-eyed expression of a sleepwalker who is only peripherally aware of what is going on.

Once the boy was curled up against his pillow and tucked under the covers, Drew rolled up the pile of clothes and placed them on the chest at the foot of the bed. He stood there for a moment, just to be sure that the boy was soundly asleep. When the boy's breathing fell into a soft rhythmic pattern, Drew turned to go.

He was at the door when the boy spoke softly yet clearly: "I don't hate you."

Drew stopped and looked back at the bed. The boy was still curled up on his side under the covers, but it was difficult to tell if he was asleep or awake. Drew waited a moment longer, and then the boy spoke again in that same soft yet clear tone of voice.

"I'm sorry for the way I treated you. You didn't deserve it. You were kind and kept your promise. And you came to rescue me even after I treated you badly."

In the silence that followed, Drew didn't know what to say. When the boy spoke again, a tremor of emotion crept into his voice.

"You are my brave and loyal knight, and I know now that you would risk your life to defend me. I know that you're not my brother . . . but you should have been. Had it been so, things would be different."

A longer silence followed, and this time Drew was pretty sure the boy had been talking in his sleep. But as he turned to go once more, the boy spoke again.

"You can't trust her."

The statement came with the force of a slap, but the figure under the covers remained motionless. Drew still wasn't sure if the boy was awake or simply talking in his sleep. According to his older brother, Drew himself used to carry on full conversations in his sleep back when he was a little kid. Drew had always believed his brother was just teasing him about the sleep-talking, but here with L in this dimly lit Hobbit-hole bedroom, he wasn't so sure anymore. And so he took a chance.

"Can't trust who?" he asked in a soft tone.

"The taller one," the boy said. "Marilyn, the quiet Elvish one. She's not who you think she is. You think she's just a pretty girl and that she would be nice to spend the night with. But she doesn't want you for just the night. Once you go with her, she'll take you to the candleroom and make you dizzy. The shorter chatty one, Danae, will think it's funny at first; then she'll say maybe they should stop. But Marilyn will tell her to leave if she doesn't like it. And when Danae is gone, Marilyn will tell you that everything is going to be all right. But it won't be all right. It will be just like it was in the scene, only for real."

The boy paused. Drew stood frozen.

"That's what she told my brother. She said it was just a scene, and that they would only do it once, and that he would like it. But they didn't do it just once. She kept wanting to do it every time. And he kept letting her do it because she was so pretty. He kept letting her push the button because she liked him more when he was dizzy."

The boy pressed the side of his face deeper into the pillow as he curled up into a tight ball under the covers. Drew went back to the bed and reached out with a tentative hand. He stroked the boy's dark hair until the rigid little frame under the covers relaxed.

For a moment, all was still and silent. Then the boy said something that gave Drew a chill.

"She'll come to you in your dreams first. She'll be gentle and loving because that's the way she always is in the beginning. But as it gets closer to Halloween, she'll change, because Halloween is the time when she takes *off* her mask and roams free . . .

"She'll call the boys to join her—the ones who were watching us from the tunnel below the ride tonight. They always come when her time is near. She likes them to watch. You needn't fear the younger ones. They're harmless. But the oldest boy is dangerous. He's more afraid of you than you are of him, because he knows that you're stronger. But you have to stay away from him. Even though he's afraid of you, he's still dangerous, and you have to stay away from him. Do you understand? She'll use the oldest boy to get to you. Do you understand?"

Drew didn't understand, but he said yes, anyway.

"Promise that you won't go to the candleroom. Promise that you won't go to her."

"I won't. I promise."

"Even in your dreams."

"Even in my dreams," Drew said, "I swear it."

It was quiet again, and for a moment Drew thought the boy might have drifted back to sleep.

Then the boy spoke one last time: "Are you still there? Would you stay with me until I fall asleep?"

Drew swallowed back the sudden lump that rose in his throat and said, "I'm still here. I'm not going anywhere."

Sometime later, Drew woke to a faint rumbling sound. At first, he thought he was dreaming, and that in his dream, he was back at the amusement park with The Silver Bullet rumbling across the stretch of tracks leading up to the highest platform of the maintenance stairs. But he wasn't dreaming. And it wasn't The Silver Bullet that had made the rumbling sound. It was one of the three garage doors opening down in the driveway below. And momentarily, that same rumbling sound came again as the huge door closed.

He'd fallen asleep in the chair next to L's bed. He wasn't sure exactly how long he'd been sleeping, but by the time displayed on the alarm clock, he guessed it had been a little over an hour. The boy was burrowed under the covers now with only a shock of that silky dark hair poking out at the top; the steady rhythm of his breathing indicated that he was fully asleep.

Drew stood and went quietly to the door. He turned to have one last look before leaving.

The upstairs hallway was silent. The door at the far end was still closed. Which was fine by Drew. Even after an hour-long rest in the chair beside L's bed, his feelings hadn't changed. He did not wish to encounter Logan. Not tonight, anyway.

He'd reached the staircase and was halfway down when a girl about his age came from the first-floor hall and stopped in the foyer when she saw him. She was stunningly beautiful, with long dark hair pulled back into a ponytail.

Though she did not have the signature smoldering grey eyes (hers were a bright and brilliant green), it was obvious at a glance that she was Logan's twin sister, Macy. She didn't seem shocked or threatened, but she was looking at him curiously, so Drew offered a nod, along with a slightly awkward smile, to let her know that he wasn't just some guy who'd walked in off the street. She returned the nod, but without a smile of her own, as if she was still waiting for Drew to explain his presence in her house after midnight.

Drew introduced himself and told her that he was a friend of Logan's from school. When Macy still didn't respond, he added, "I put your little brother to bed and tucked him in. He asked me to stay until he fell asleep." He laughed a short, awkward laugh. "I guess I dozed off myself. He's fine, though. He's sound asleep now. We had a long night. He's a tough kid, but I think he's worn out."

Macy responded with an unexpected laugh and a curious half-smile. "Oooooh-kay," she said, shaking her head lightly. "Not sure I needed that much information, but that's cool. I'm glad you two had a good time."

Drew looked confused.

Macy waved an apologetic hand and shook her head with a self-deprecating "pay no attention to that bitch behind the curtain" smile. As she passed him on the stairs, she said, "Well, it was nice to meet you, Drew. Any friend of my little brother's is a friend of mine. Would you mind making sure the door is locked on your way out? It sticks sometimes, and the latch doesn't catch."

She disappeared around the corner of the upstairs hallway before Drew even had the chance to say, "It was nice meeting you, too," or "Goodnight." He just stood there on the staircase for a moment, nonplussed. There had been something odd in the way she'd hit the words "little brother." A sarcastic lilt in her tone, though not snide. It came off more like a teasing verbal wink, as if she and Drew had both been in on the same joke.

Drew was still trying to make sense of the odd exchange with Macy on the stairs when he reached his car and looked up at Logan's window. The room was still dark, but he thought he could see the shadowy outline of a figure standing there behind the drawn sheers. Drew waited for a moment to see if Logan would step up into the moonlight that shone down on his window. But when the outline of the figure—if indeed it was there at all—didn't move, Drew unlocked his car door and got inside. He was done playing games with Logan. For now, at least.

He fired up the engine and headed down the long driveway to the main road. And as the huge house became smaller and smaller in his rearview mirror, Drew felt a curious chill. And with this chill, the words the boy, L, had shouted atop the roller coaster tracks came flooding back to him . . .

I'm alone here! I'm the only one left! You're not here! You're not real! None of this is real!

And pressing close behind, the words L had whispered to him up in the room before they had both drifted off to sleep . . .

She'll come to you in your dreams . . . she'll be gentle and loving . . . but as it gets closer to Halloween, she'll change, because Halloween is the time when she takes off her mask and roams free . . . she'll call the boys . . . they always come when her time is near . . . you needn't fear the younger ones . . . but the oldest boy is dangerous . . . you have to stay away from him . . . you have to stay away from her *. . . promise that you won't go to her.*

Though he'd been certain that the outburst atop the roller coaster tracks had been nothing more than a cry for attention from an angry and frustrated boy, Drew could not say the same for what he'd heard in the quiet bedroom after tucking the boy in. It was the softly whispered entreaty . . . *promise that you won't go to her . . .* which resonated now.

It had not been the stubborn demand of an angry and frustrated kid seeking attention. It had been the desperate plea of a terrified boy.

But the boy hadn't been afraid for his *own* safety.

He had been afraid for *Drew's* safety.

And that gave rise to all sorts of questions . . . ones that would gnaw at Drew until he had all the answers.

ACT THREE
THROUGH THE WINDOW

A T FIRST, IT WAS QUIET.
     Then they both spoke at once.
"Is it true?"

"I can explain."

It wasn't funny, like in the movies when two characters speak at the same time. It was awkward and frustrating, and for an uncomfortable interval, neither of them spoke. They just continued to stare at one another across the little corner table at the back of the coffee shop.

Drew waited a measured moment, then repeated the question in an even tone: "Is it true?"

Logan remained calm, his eyes, as always, unreadable. Drew waited, but his patience was wearing thin. He'd discovered a lot over the past week—much of it inexplicable, most of it disturbing—and he wanted more than facile answers. He wanted the truth.

Logan touched his coffee cup and said, "I'm not sure where to begin."

Drew said flatly, "Why don't you start with the girls at

the amusement park—Marilyn and Danae—you know, the ones that have been dead for the past seven years."

Logan offered a small, rueful half smile. "I don't think you're ready for that."

"You'd be surprised what I'm ready for," Drew said with a hard glare.

Logan nodded, but his eyes looked distant. "You may be right."

"Or maybe you'd like to start with the kid that you talked into playing the part of your 'little brother.'" Drew was unable to suppress the disgust in his tone. "I'll give you points for casting. He looks just like you. Where did you find him? Is one of your mommy's rich friends an agent or a casting director? Did it cost a lot? Of course, money wouldn't be a concern for you, right? Not in the pursuit of your big scene."

Drew uttered a bitter laugh. Logan sipped his coffee.

"I should have known the whole thing was a setup," Drew said, shaking his head at his own naiveté. "You and your scenes—what bullshit." He gave a humorless chuckle. "The kid was very good, by the way—L. He didn't break character once. Very talented little actor. You should give him a bonus."

"He wasn't acting," Logan said. "He's real—"

Drew brought his fist down hard on the table and snapped, "You don't *have* a little brother!"

An older woman sitting at a table near the front window looked over at them. Drew lowered his voice, but his eyes remained firmly fixed on Logan. He was determined to see this through.

"You *had* an *older* brother—who apparently was a real psycho, just like you. No, wait. You haven't *killed* anybody yet. You just like to set up sick little reenactment scenes. Yeah, I read all about your brother online, the way he liked to O.D. on his insulin and then get creative with a knife on your babysitter. *Marilyn*. You know, the *real* Marilyn." He laughed that same bitter laugh. "Again, excellent casting. Your girl at the amusement park could have been her twin. I'm not sure about that Danae girl—you know, the one who offed herself with sleeping pills a few weeks after your brother killed her best friend—because they didn't have any pictures of her online, but I'm sure you spared no expense to find a reasonable look-a-like to play her, too. I guess I'd be flattered that you went to such extreme lengths just to impress me—that is, if the whole thing wasn't so disgustingly twisted, you know? And let's face it, this is some pretty twisted shit. Even for a certifiable freak like you."

Logan's gaze didn't waver. Nor did Drew's.

"Tell me something," Drew said. "That kid you hired to play the part of L—" He cut himself off and smiled bitterly. "Clever touch, by the way—'L' for Logan. I didn't catch that one at all, at least not until after I'd figured out the rest of it. I take it he was supposed to be you, and I was supposed to be your older brother. Am I right?"

Logan remained silent. Drew pressed on—he was well past the point of being put off by Logan's silences.

"That's what all the run around at the amusement park was about, right? Little Brother finally gets some quality time with Big Brother, who's been dissing him off. That is, until the girls show up in line for the ride and Big Brother turns his back on little brother once again. Then Little Brother takes off, forcing Big Brother to realize his mistake and race around in a desperate search for the little guy. Very smooth. And I did exactly what you expected me to do."

Drew grit his teeth and shook his head. Logan had set up a life-sized maze, complete with all manner of twists and turns and hurdles and traps, and Drew had raced through it like a dutiful mouse. But the humiliation over being so easily led through that maze was nothing compared to the anger that had risen in its wake.

Drew had willingly agreed to do Logan's multilayered scene and could not deny his genuine curiosity to see where the whole thing was headed. The scene with the two guys in the bedroom, one shooting multiple doses of insulin into the other until he passes out, had been more intriguing than frightening. Even the bit with the gun and the crazy talk hadn't turned Drew off. It was just play acting—convincing and creepy play acting, but nothing that went too far.

But the follow-up scene with the kid brother—an actual kid, who could have been seriously injured or killed that night atop the roller coaster tracks—*that* scene *had* gone too far. If the boy had failed to reach out to Drew at precisely the right moment, if Drew had failed to catch hold of him and pull him onto the safety of the maintenance platform in time, Logan's little "living theatre" experiment would have ended in a very real tragedy.

Just *thinking* about what might have happened at the amusement park last Friday made Drew's blood course with anger. The sensation only intensified with the orchestrator of that little slice of terror sitting across the table from him, casually sipping coffee, as if the two of them were merely discussing the next phase of the "scene."

"Tell me," Drew said, "do his parents know what you got their kid to do for you that night? Forget about all the dialogue you wrote for him to say—shit that no little kid should be saying. Do they know that he stood on the tracks of a roller coaster and almost got killed? Did you tell him to do that? Or was he just supposed to wait for me at the top of the maintenance stairs, and then decided on his own to 'improvise' at the last second?"

Drew paused and gave Logan an oddly friendly smile. Logan remained silent.

"Because," Drew continued in a paradoxically pleasant tone, "if you tell me that you *did* instruct that little kid to step out onto those tracks with a speeding roller coaster coming at him, I'm going to get up, take you by the throat, and punch you repeatedly in the face until you drop. So, you'll want to be very careful how you answer the question because I'm dead serious."

Logan looked at Drew for a moment. Though his countenance appeared pleasant, even friendly, there was no trace of humor in Drew's eyes; he was indeed dead serious.

Logan maintained eye contact when he said, "I didn't tell him to get on the tracks."

"But you did tell him to go up the steps to the top."

"No."

"*Don't* you fuckin' lie to me," Drew spat through gritted teeth.

"I'm not lying to you," Logan said calmly. "I didn't tell him to go up the steps. I didn't tell him to get on the tracks. And I didn't write any dialogue for him to say. I didn't even know he was with you that night . . . until it was over."

"Bullshit. You put him up to it. Everything that kid did, everything he said that night came from you. I know how you talk. I know the games you play. I know the way you get under someone's skin and mess with their mind—"

"'His' mind," Logan corrected. "You know the way I

get under someone's skin and mess with 'his' mind—not 'their' mind."

"Just like that," Drew said with a smile that bordered on a snarl. "Here, answer this one for me, Professor Grammar-and-Syntax. Who wrote the note that was on the kitchen counter? You know, the one about the second phase of the scene, with all the rules for me to follow. Who wrote that note and left it there for me?"

Logan took another sip of his coffee and set the cup back on the table. "L wrote it."

Drew shook his head with an incredulous laugh. "Dude, you're either an amazing actor, or you really *are* insane. *I* almost believe you, and I *know* you're full of shit."

The older woman sitting near the front window gave them a reproachful glance as she got up and left the coffee shop. Drew didn't seem to notice. He was far too focused on Logan.

After a moment, Drew said, "OK. At the risk of feeding your perverse little fantasy, I'll play along. L wrote the note and planned the whole thing from the start, without any help or coercion from you. He's just a 'really real' ten-year-old kid who just *happened* to be in your house the night you and I were supposed to get together to do the second part of your bullshit drama class scene . . . which is an amazement in itself because you are *not* in any of the drama classes at our school—I checked your schedule in the main office, so don't even bother lying about it. But that's beside the point, so we'll just stick with the night in question and pretend, for the sake of argument, that you're not completely full of shit." He paused and gave Logan a smile that was anything but pleasant. "Let's just cut straight to the chase instead. Who is this mysterious kid L who has access to your house, the keys to your expensive SUV, and an unlimited credit card in your name?" He chuckled and added, "Oh, yeah, and he also speaks fluent French—that was a good touch, must have taken weeks of rehearsal. But again, that's not the point. The point is, if he's not an actor you hired—and we *know* he's not your little brother—who is he?"

Logan looked unmoved by Drew's ire. He ran a steady finger along the rim of his coffee cup and said, "You wouldn't believe me if I told you."

"Try me."

"You're not ready to hear the truth."

"Oh, I'm ready," Drew said, with a humorless chuckle. "Let's hear it. Let's hear you speak the truth for once. I double-dog dare you to speak one word of the truth. Tell me who L is. Tell me the truth, and I'll believe you."

"I'll tell you, but you still won't believe me."

"If it's the truth, I will."

Logan looked up at the clock on the wall above the service counter. He watched as the second hand made its way around the face of the clock, a full 360 degrees, before turning his gaze back to Drew. In that single minute, something had shifted in his cool grey eyes, something deep and distant, as if a part of him that was there just sixty seconds ago was now gone, and his eyes suddenly looked a little haunted. He took a short breath and spoke.

"To understand what I'm about to say—to fully grasp it—you'd need to have at least a basic understanding of quantum physics and the theory of parallel universes."

"Well, then you've already lost me," Drew said, without hesitation. "I'm just a dumb jock, in case you forgot, so you'd better simplify it for me."

Logan could see that Drew would never believe him,

but he had to give it a try. There really was no turning back at this point. He exhaled a short, even breath and looked steadily into Drew's eyes.

"With every second we live, every action we produce—no matter how great or small—we leave an imprint on time, like a fingerprint on a glass, or a footprint in the snow. Only these impressions can't be rubbed out or washed away. Once they're imprinted on the fabric of time, they're there to stay. Most people think of them as memories, like the mother who can still hear the running footsteps and echoing laughter of her kids long after they've grown up and moved on to their own lives. This is because those kids never really left. They're still there in that house, or on the playground, or at the mall, or even at the amusement park during Terror Fest. Their *imprints* are indelible. They can never be erased."

Logan paused. Drew waited.

"Some people—" Logan continued, "—people who are exceptionally receptive—can pick up on these imprints, and depending on the strength of the imprint itself, past and present can sometimes intersect, allowing a receptive person to interact with an imprint. There have been several documented cases of this phenomenon. In particular, one where a ninety-three-year-old Armenian man approached a vacationing family from France and, with tears in his eyes, thanked their sixteen-year-old son for saving him from Turkish soldiers when he, the old man, was only six years old. The sixteen-year-old French kid had been out sightseeing on his own just two days before when he'd come across a lost Armenian boy and helped him find his way safely home. At first, the French family thought the old man was thanking their son for helping out his grandson, but the old man insisted that the French teen had rescued *him*. The teen told his parents that he hadn't seen any soldiers in pursuit of the boy. But he contended that the rest of the details of the old man's story were indeed accurate, and he swore that the old man's eyes looked exactly like the eyes of the little boy he'd rescued just two days before."

Logan paused again, but this time Drew didn't wait for him to continue.

"So you're telling me that the kid I met in your house last Friday—the kid I went to dinner and the amusement park with—L—was an . . . imprint?"

Logan remained silent. Drew pressed on.

"For the sake of argument, let's say that I believe you. That everything you've said is actually possible, that I'm a 'receptor' for imprints—that would be the right way to put it, right? I can see people who imprinted themselves on the past—"

"Not just any people—"

"Right," Drew said with a sarcastically sweet lilt, "just this L kid who hangs out at your house and builds domino pyramids and likes to climb out onto the tracks of roller coasters for kicks. Anyway, let's say I buy all this crap. Lock, stock, and barrel. I'm all in. If this kid was just an imprint—and we'll forget the fact that I held him in my arms, that I carried him up the stairs at your house and got him into his pyjamas and tucked him into bed, which is really something, considering he's just a figment of my imagination—"

"I never said that."

"Right, cos he's a 'really real' boy who came to life just so I could save him—which was very nice of him to do because we both know that I'm the hero in this scene of yours—"

"I never said that either."

"But it would be *implied* since I'm the one who climbed to the top of a roller coaster to save that kid from getting *killed.*"

Drew's gaze hardened as he emphasized the last word. He wanted Logan to show a sign of emotion—a flicker of fear, of guilt, or remorse, over risking the life of a little kid for the sake of his own sick amusement. But again, there was no reaction from Logan. Just that infuriatingly calm grey gaze.

"So," Drew said, "if this kid was just an imprint of the past, as you say, how come other people could see him? I mean, I get that *I* could see him—me being a 'receptor' and all, right? But how could *other* people see him? Those two girls at the amusement park, the waiter at the restaurant— are they all receptors too? That'd be a real coincidence—four receptors all crossing paths in the same night. Pretty wild, even by *your* nutty standards, wouldn't you agree?" Drew smiled bitterly. "Go ahead, take your time coming up with an explanation for that one. I'm your captive audience."

Logan looked down at his coffee. "I think you already know why the girls could see L."

Drew's eyes lit up, and he chuckled. "That's right. You got me. They're *ghosts.* I hadn't thought of that. Makes sense, though. They're both dead. One committed suicide, and your older brother killed the other one."

Logan flinched, but Drew didn't seem to notice.

"So," Drew continued, "I'm gonna take a wild stab in the dark here and guess that *you* are the mysterious kid L— or that L is the 'imprint' you left behind from your screwed up childhood." He paused and shifted gears. "Not that it matters, but why 'L?'"

"That's what he used to call me."

"Your older brother?"

Logan nodded, but his eyes looked distant and lost. For a moment, Drew almost felt sorry for him. But then he chuckled again and shook his head.

"Man, you've got this act down cold, don't you? I assume you've also got it all figured out just why the ghosts of these girls happened to show up at the amusement park the very same night your little 'imprint' and I were there— and believe me, I can't wait to hear all about it. I'm sure it's gonna be a wild one. But first, I'm dying to know how the waiter at the restaurant was able to see your imprint. Is he a receptor, like me? Or just a really good actor, like the rest of your little ensemble?"

Logan ignored the quip and spoke plainly. "No. Olivier was a waiter. He was always very kind to me, and eventually, my mother hired him part-time to tutor me in French. He was killed in a car accident back when I was still a kid."

There was a moment of silence. Then Drew snapped his fingers—a sharp and sudden sound that made Logan blink—and a grin broke out across his face as he shook his head.

"Of course! The waiter was a ghost *too*—a *friendly* ghost. Now it *all* makes sense. Was the food he served ghost food? Because it sure tasted pretty real to me."

Logan's eyes iced over, but then he reeled in the emotion and said, "It was real."

"Yeah," Drew said with a nod, "because ghosts can get into the kitchen to get the food without anybody noticing them. I forgot about that. Makes sense." He chuckled again. "This stuff is really great. It doesn't require a shred of proof to back it up. You can just make up the rules as you go along to fit whatever bullshit you come up with. I gotta hand it to you, the French tutor part was almost moving. Did you ever consider asking him to play the part of your big brother?" Drew smacked his forehead with the heel of his hand. "Oh, wait, I almost forgot. *You're* not Olivier's type. He prefers American jocks like me, right?"

Though his cheeks burned with shame, Logan did not avert his gaze from Drew. "I'm sorry I offended you. I shouldn't have said that. It was insensitive and rude."

"Oh, no offense," Drew said mockingly. "I mean, it wasn't really *you*, anyway, right? It was *L*. And he's just a little kid—or the 'imprint' of a little kid, right? But that *does* bring up a curious point. If it was your imprint I spent that night with, how do you know what was said between me and L and Olivier? I mean, an imprint is its own entity, right? In your own words, once you move on, your imprint just stays there, like 'fingerprints on a glass' or 'footsteps in the snow.'" He paused briefly, and his eyes became deadly serious. "So, how do you know what your imprint said and did that night with me?"

Logan was unperturbed by the attempt to trap him. "Both the subject and his imprint are living entities, separate yet connected. Anything the imprint experiences automatically becomes a memory for the subject."

Drew tilted his head back and smiled with narrowed eyes like a curious pupil on the verge of almost believing a story well beyond the realm of believability. Then he uttered a soundless half-laugh.

"I have to give it to you, man. You've got this thing covered from every possible angle." He shook his head in genuine wonder. "It is absolutely mind-boggling how deep you're willing to go with this thing. I mean, most guys would have given up by now and just admitted the truth, but you—"

"It is the truth," Logan said.

Drew froze and looked deeply into Logan's eyes, searching for a chink in the armor, a flicker of doubt, but there was nothing to indicate that Logan was lying. It occurred to Drew that Logan might *not* be acting, that he might actually *believe* all these wild stories about imprints and ghosts. Maybe the guy really *was* crazy, like Coach had said. Drew had spoken to Coach a few days after the whole amusement park incident, and Coach had filled him in on the story of Logan's older brother, Martyn, and the babysitter, Marilyn. Coach didn't have all the details. All he knew was that seven years ago on Halloween night, Martyn Kōtarō stabbed his younger brother's babysitter to death and was shot dead by the police while still holding the bloody hunting knife.

Drew had found more information online. Martyn and Marilyn were both seventeen and went to the same school. According to friends, the two had been dating for about five months before that tragic Halloween night. Marilyn's body was discovered in her upstairs bedroom. There was no evidence of sexual assault, but saliva samples taken from the mouths of both the victim and her killer indicated that they had been intimate shortly before the murder. During their search of the house, police officers found ten-year-old Logan curled up into a ball at the back of a closet in the bedroom where the murder had taken place. It wasn't clear if the boy had witnessed the murder, but the blood smears on his face, hands, and clothes indicated that he had been in contact with the body. According to the police report, the small handprints on the victim's arms were consistent with the coroner's assertion that the victim's body had been moved slightly from where it had landed on the floor at the point of death, as if someone had attempted to revive the victim by shaking her.

But even more disturbing—if anything could possibly be more disturbing than a brutal knife murder of a seventeen-year-old girl—was the condition of the closet door. It was littered with slash marks made by the same knife that had been used to kill Marilyn. More than thirty penetrating gashes, but the door had held up, and the boy inside had survived the bloody night.

Drew had thought about that a lot over the days leading up to this meeting with Logan. He had thought about the frightened little boy trapped in that closet while his older brother, who'd just killed his babysitter, stabbed at the door to get at him. Drew couldn't imagine anything more horrifying than being attacked by someone you loved, someone you relied on to protect you. He couldn't imagine what it must have been like for Logan cringing inside that dark closet as the blade of the hunting knife stabbed through the door.

Drew remembered the photograph he'd seen of the two brothers on the shelf in the gaming room at Logan's house. The night he'd met L. At the time, he'd believed it to be a recent shot of Logan and L. But he'd since discovered that it was, in fact, a seven-year-old photo of Martyn at seventeen and Logan at ten. The resemblance between the two boys in that photo had been uncanny. But even more uncanny was that Logan had grown up to be a near exact physical replica of his older brother: the same silky dark locks overhanging the haunting grey eyes, the same strikingly handsome features . . . the same deceptively lean frame of a guy who possessed more than enough strength to drive the blade of a knife through a sturdy closet door . . .

In his mind, Drew pictured the culmination of that terrifying night seven years ago, as if it were a scene from a horror movie . . . the hunting knife, streaked with blood, penetrating the closet door . . . splinters of wood raining down on the frightened little boy inside . . . the sound of approaching sirens in the distance. According to one of the articles he'd read online, someone had placed a call to 911 from inside the house; the recording was filled with bursts of static, punctuated by loud hammer-like noises, which were later identified as the repeated blows of the knife driving through the closet door.

The only portion of the caller's plea that had come through with crystal clarity was at the end, just before the line went dead. A single phrase cried out twice by a young boy in holy terror: " . . . *she's here!* . . . *she's here!*"

According to people who'd heard a leaked copy of the 911 recording on fuzzbuzz.net—before it had been pulled by the site's admin—those two words repeated in that terrified shriek had sent chills up their spines.

The voice of the caller had been positively identified as Logan's. He'd placed the call from Marilyn's mobile phone while crouched down at the back of the closet. It was this image—the image of a frightened ten-year-old boy calling for help while his older brother stabbed wildly at the closet door with a knife—that rose in Drew's head now and remained long enough to cool his temper. Long enough to make him feel something other than anger for the guy sitting across the table from him.

Drew sighed and said, "I want to understand you. I wouldn't have agreed to meet you here otherwise. I know what you've been through, and I'm not going to pretend that I could even begin to know what that must have been like . . . with your brother and all. But I want to understand you."

"I don't need your understanding," Logan said with an edge in his voice. "And I don't need your pity. You can be angry at me for what you think I've put you through; I deserve that much. What happened with you and L that night at the amusement park is entirely on me. I never should have invited you back to my house. Even though it was you who approached me on the soccer pitch that morning, it was still my call, and I should have known better. I should have never let you weasel your way back in. I should have told you to slag off and been done with it right then and there."

Drew looked as if he'd been slapped or spit on. His jaw went tight, and his nostrils flared. But Logan wasn't finished.

"You say you want to understand, but you're not even willing to listen. That's your right as well, I reckon. I'm not sure that *I* would believe me, were our positions reversed." Here, Logan's eyes suddenly went a shade darker. "But don't you *ever* presume to make assumptions about my brother. You didn't know him, and you have no right to speak ill of the dead. *I* have that right because, unlike you, *I* know the dead . . . and I understand the threat she poses to the living. A real threat that you seem more than content to ignore, at your own peril." He took a short breath. "My brother was a hero that night. He *saved* me, much the same as you saved L on the tracks of the roller coaster. He was a hero who never harmed a soul in his entire life."

Drew suddenly snapped. "He killed your babysitter!"

Logan gave a bitter half-smile. "And it happened on Halloween." He paused. Then, with no sign of sarcasm, he said, "Don't believe everything you hear. Even when it comes from supposedly reliable sources."

Drew shook his head in confusion. Logan's gaze remained cool and fixed.

"My *brother* didn't kill anyone," Logan said flatly. He paused briefly, and then said something completely unexpected: "It was me . . . or, if you prefer, L. Either way, it's the same difference: *I'm* the one who killed Marilyn."

Drew sat frozen in place. It was as if he were back on the Hell-evator, strapped in and waiting for the mechanism to release the suspended seat and send him plunging down the side of the spire at breakneck speed.

But the drop never came.

He just hung up there, where the air was thin and cold, as wave upon wave of blood crashed at his temples in a dizzying series of slow-driving throbs, like the hammering pulse of some massive mythical beast.

"I can understand your shock," Logan said calmly. "But if you'll allow it, I can explain. It's not quite what you're thinking. It's more . . . complicated."

Drew remained perfectly still, suspended at that towering height, still waiting for the fall.

"You need to understand that my former au pair wasn't quite the angel portrayed in the myriad articles you've undoubtedly discovered online. She was, in fact, quite the opposite. Though not inherently wicked—at least not until that Halloween night—Marilyn possessed certain . . . abilities. Nothing like what you see in movies or on TV. She couldn't set someone on fire with her eyes or use telekinesis to flip over buses, or anything like that. She didn't chant spells over a cauldron or fly on a broomstick either.

"But she *did* possess certain powers, among them the ability to make you see things that weren't actually there. You've experienced this little phenomenon firsthand, that night at the amusement park when you and L got on the Hell-evator. The three boys standing in the tunnel. Do you remember L telling you that they weren't really there, that they were just imaginary, and to open your eyes and they would go away? And it worked, didn't it? When you opened your eyes, they were gone, weren't they?"

Drew felt himself nodding from that place where he remained suspended, still waiting for the imminent fall, and Logan went on.

"She could also get you to *do* things . . . things that you would never dream of doing under normal circumstances . . . like stepping onto the tracks of a roller coaster."

There was a flicker in Drew's eyes, just a tiny one, but Logan caught it and nodded grimly. He took a measured breath before continuing.

"On that particular Halloween—the night she died— she used that power on me. She'd had an argument with Martyn. He'd come over to her house, where she was baby-sitting me. Normally, she would have come to our house to sit for both my sister and me, but my sister was at a sleepover, and Marilyn felt bad for me not being able to go because it was an all-girls thing. So she suggested we go trick-or-treating twice, first in my neighborhood and then in hers. My mother had picked out a Jedi Knight costume for me. But Marilyn knew that I really wanted to go as Eric Draven in *The Crow*. I wore the Jedi costume in my neighborhood, but when we got to Marilyn's house, she told me that she had a surprise for me. And she did. She'd made a Crow costume, and it looked exactly like the one in the movie.

"I was changing costumes when Martyn showed up. I was up in Marilyn's room, but the door was open, and I could hear them talking downstairs in the foyer. After a while, I crept out into the hall and peeked over the banister. They were down there kissing, which wasn't odd. I'd seen them kissing many times before. Only this time . . . something was different. This time, Martyn didn't seem to be enjoying the moment. He kept pulling back gently and telling her to hold on a second. He said that he had to tell her something . . . something important. But she just kept touching him and laughing and saying, 'You know you like it.'"

Logan stopped. His grey eyes seemed to darken at the memory. He took a short breath and went on.

"But Martyn *didn't* like it. I could tell by the look in his eyes and the way he kept taking her hands off his chest. He *didn't* like it, and he wanted her to stop and listen to him. But she just kept touching his chest and his arms and his hair, and laughing this really beautiful laugh, the sort that would make any guy fall in love with her.

"But that was just it. Martyn wasn't *any* guy, and he wasn't in love with her anymore. I could see it in his eyes. And eventually, Marilyn saw it too.

"And that's when things changed. That's when everything changed. Martyn told her that he didn't like the things they'd been doing, the messing around with his insulin dispenser and getting him all dizzy. He said it made him feel sick. And it had. I'd seen it in his eyes at breakfast on mornings after he'd been with Marilyn and her friend Danae. I'd almost told our mother about it a few times—I *should* have told her—but Martyn had sworn me to secrecy. He told me that it wasn't as bad as it looked and that he was all right. But he wasn't all right. It was making him sick, and I was afraid that it might end up killing him. I'm pretty sure that Danae was afraid, too, because after a while, she'd stopped showing up when Marilyn came round to babysit my sister and me.

"But Marilyn wasn't afraid of it—she wasn't afraid of anything. It amused her, and no one was going to interfere with any pursuit that gave Marilyn amusement, not even my brother, whom she claimed to love with all her heart."

Logan closed his eyes and took a calming breath, which appeared to help because when he opened them, the darkness that had been there only moments before was gone. But the bitterness still flashed behind those sharp eyes, like tiny bolts of lightning scarcely contained by twin grey storm clouds. In his mind, Logan could hear a voice echoing from the deep recesses of his memory . . .

You must do as I say.

It was a gentle and familiar voice—that of his ten-year-old self, L. And it was followed by the voice of his older brother.

Just make sure to stop before I slip into a coma, OK? You need to make sure to give me the soda to bring my levels back up. Do you understand?

Logan wasn't sure now if he *had* understood. Not fully, anyway. Was it possible to make yourself believe something, even when you knew it wasn't true? Then he recalled the image of Marilyn, the power she'd held over his older brother—*she had bewitched him*—and he thought, yes, it is possible to make yourself believe something, even if you know it isn't true. Martyn had believed. Right up until the end, when the spell was broken and the truth stood starkly naked before him. But by then it was too late. Too late to save Martyn, who was good and kind and brave, and had never harmed a soul.

Logan felt tears threaten, but he willed them not to fall. He held his resolve because there was still time to save Drew. He forced himself to believe that this was possible and that he could actually do it. He *would* do it. Because Drew had been kind and gentle to L, even after the boy had treated him so badly. He had proven himself worthy when he risked his life to save L . . . and in doing so, he had saved Logan, too. Because if L had been killed on the roller coaster tracks that night, it stood to reason that Logan himself would have ceased to exist. Drew had saved him, and he had to at least *try* to save Drew.

But to succeed with Drew where he had failed with Martyn, he would have to accomplish a near-impossible feat. He would have to make Drew believe. Not as an actor playing a part in a scene—the time for play acting was over—but as a friend who was in very real danger. And to do this, Logan would have to tell the truth . . . or at least as much of it as he possibly could without revealing things that would send the guy running straight for the exit.

Logan took another breath and went on: "Once Marilyn realized that Martyn was serious, that he didn't want to be her boyfriend anymore, her demeanor changed. She didn't yell or cry. Quite the opposite, in fact; she seemed perfectly calm. She told him that she needed to get back to me, that we were going trick-or-treating, and that we'd be back in a few hours. She said she would appreciate it if Martyn would come back to collect me round ten.

"Martyn left then, and I slipped back into the room so that Marilyn wouldn't know I'd been listening by the banister. She smiled like her old self when she saw me in the Crow costume she'd made, and at first, I thought everything was going to be fine. Marilyn seemed genuinely happy as we went from door to door, collecting treats—but like I said, she had a way of making you see what she wanted you to see. It was her gift.

"It wasn't until we'd come to the last street in her neighborhood that the mask of her smile began to fade, and by the time we got back to her house, the tears she'd been holding at bay all night began to fall. I put my arms around her and held her as she cried. I wanted to be strong for her. I wanted to make her tears go away and bring back her smile, but I didn't know how to do it. Only Martyn could do that. I'd seen him do it when she was feeling sad before. He would take her in his arms and kiss her tears away. He would tell her that everything was going to be all right, and she would believe him because she could see into his soul and knew that he was honest and would never lie to her.

"I knew that I could never be like Martyn, but I tried. I held her tight and told her that everything was going to be all right. I told her that I would do whatever it took to make everything all right, and as the warmth of her embrace encompassed me, I could hear her speaking. Not aloud, but inside my head. She told me that there was something I *could* do, and if I was brave enough and strong enough, that I could make everything all right. And suddenly I felt very brave and strong—braver and stronger than even

Martyn—and everything seemed very clear to me. I somehow knew exactly what needed to be done, and further, that *I* was the only one who could do it.

"I was waiting in the living room when Martyn came to collect me. He let himself in, as he always did, and found me standing in the darkened room, with the light of the fireplace burning behind me. He asked if I was ready to go, and I shook my head. I told him that I needed him to do something for me first. I think he thought I was joking because he smiled this curious smile, but he had been out drinking with his mates, and I could see that he was still a little buzzed. He asked what I wanted, and when I told him, he laughed. He looked round and asked where Marilyn was. I told him that she wasn't feeling well and had gone to bed. That made his smile fade. He felt bad about the way he'd treated her—Martyn always became a little maudlin after one too many drinks. He said that maybe he should go up to see her, and I concurred. But I told him that first, he would have to do as I say. That made him smile and laugh again—he always found it amusing when I stood up to him, especially when he'd been drinking.

"I could hear Marilyn speaking inside my head as the fire crackled behind me—*it's just a scene, like in a movie or a play, and everything will be wonderful after, trust me*—and I told Martyn to get down on his knees. He smiled that same half-drunk smile and did as he was told. I felt a strange surge of power when he let me tie his hands behind his back, the same way he'd let the girls do so many times before—and just as Marilyn had instructed, I took care not to tie the rope too tightly, so that Martyn would be able to wriggle free when the time came. I wasn't sure whether the tiny wave of delirium that accompanied this surge was coming from my own thoughts or the thoughts that Marilyn had placed inside my head, but either way, it felt good and just. Even as the desperate voice of reason deep inside me cried out that it was all wrong, I couldn't resist the magnetic pull of the greater force within. I could see my hand, as if it wasn't even attached to my arm, reaching out for the little black box clipped to Martyn's belt. I could feel my finger on the button. But it was more like something out of a dream . . .

"And then Martyn reminded me that I would have to make sure to stop before he slipped into a coma. He told me to make sure to give him the soda to bring his levels back up to normal and asked if I understood this.

"I think I nodded—I must have because Martyn was smiling that buzzed smile again, like he was proud of me. Of course, at that point, he had no clue that he had less than an hour left to live."

Logan's eyes suddenly brimmed with bitter tears, and he stopped speaking. It took him a moment to compose himself, and then he continued.

"He didn't die from an overdose of the insulin, as you already know. I only pushed the button ten or eleven times, enough to get him woozy, but not enough to put him into a coma. Just as she wanted. She wanted him to be able to get up the stairs when she started screaming. She wanted him to see what his actions had wrought.

"She called to me as Martyn slumped to the floor. I left him there sideways, and ascended the stairs, toward that place at the top, where the three boys stood, waiting and watching like sentinels. I wasn't afraid of them as I'd been before. I knew she had called them to join us and that they were only there to observe and learn.

"She was waiting for me in the bedroom with the knife. She told me it wasn't a real knife, that it was simply a prop for our scene. *Our magnificent scene, Logan*—she never referred to me as L, even when speaking inside my head. She told me to take the knife and do what we had rehearsed. She said there would appear to be blood—a great deal of blood—but not to worry, because we both knew that she had the talent of making things appear that weren't really there at all. She smiled and told me to take the knife, that everything would be wonderful again . . . "

Logan's eyes appeared to crackle with a sudden surge of electricity, a hopeful light within that faded as quickly as it came.

"By the time I came back to myself, Marilyn was lying on the floor—and as she'd promised, there was a lot of blood. I grabbed her arms and shook her, begging her to make it all disappear. But it didn't disappear. Because it wasn't something she'd conjured, like the three imaginary boys. It was real. I had stabbed her more than a dozen times with the knife. I had no memory of doing this, but the knife was in my hand when I came back to myself. I heard it fall to the floor just before I grabbed her arms and began to shake her.

"I think my mind went blank for a while because the next thing I remember was being in the closet. I don't remember locking it, but I must have. I wanted to get away from her. I remember thinking, *You have to get away from her, run, hide.* But I couldn't really hide, because she was out of her body now, and a locked door couldn't keep her out . . . the dead have ways of getting in—even as a child, I understood this.

"And in the darkness of that closet, I suddenly knew that I was no longer alone. I must have grabbed her mobile before going into the closet because it was in my hand. I don't remember dialing, but suddenly the voice of an emergency operator was speaking, telling me that they had received the text message I'd sent earlier and that an ambulance and officers were already on their way. For a moment, I thought I'd gone mad because I hadn't *sent* an emergency text message.

"It didn't become clear to me until later that it was Marilyn who'd sent the emergency text *before* we'd begun her little 'scene.' She'd called for the ambulance beforehand to make sure that they would get there in time to save her. She'd known that the moment Martyn heard her scream, he would break free of the rope and come racing up to her room. I can only assume that from there she would tell him to pull the knife out of her, so that her blood would be on his hands and his fingerprints would be on the knife. I don't believe that she'd intended anything more than a few superficial wounds—just enough to make it look as though Martyn had attacked her in a drunken fit. And if I tried to explain the truth, who would believe the word of a traumatized kid who'd just witnessed the brutal stabbing of his babysitter by the older brother he idolized and adored? They would simply believe that I was trying to cover up for Martyn.

"Save for that one fatal misstep, everything had gone precisely as she'd planned. Martyn heard the scream, broke free of his bonds, and came rushing upstairs. I could hear the faint sound of sirens in the distance, but by then I was trembling fiercely because I could feel her cold breath at my neck. Then her lips close to my ear, whispering . . . and that's when I started to scream . . . "

She's here! . . . she's here! Drew thought, with a sudden chill, recalling what he'd read about that night online.

" . . . and then I could hear Martyn on the other side of the door. He was shouting at Marilyn's body, *'What have you done? My god, what have you done?'*

"I cried out to Martyn from inside the closet. He tried to get the door open, but it was locked. I wanted to reach up and unlock it, but I couldn't. I just stayed there on the floor with my knees pulled up to my chest and my arms wrapped around my legs, trembling, too frightened to reach for the handle.

"Then I could hear Martyn pounding on the door, kicking at it, throwing his shoulder into it, but it was solid and didn't give. That's when he took up the knife and began to stab at the door to break it open. He wasn't trying to kill me—he was trying to *save* me. But all the police saw when they burst into Marilyn's room with their guns drawn was a dead girl on the floor in a pool of her own blood and a half-crazed-looking teenager stabbing at a locked closet door, where inside a little boy who'd placed a desperate call to 911 cried out in holy terror."

A long silence followed the tale.

Then, finally, Drew spoke, his voice soft yet clear. "Are you finished?"

Logan's staid features shifted into an expression of mild curiosity. It was only when Drew continued in the same soft tone that Logan noticed the shadow of fear behind his eyes.

"Because, if you're finished . . . I'd really like to go."

"You think I'm dangerous now," Logan said calmly.

"I didn't say that. I just want to go." His body tensed as if readying for a fight, should the need arise, but the fear still lingered just beneath the surface of his eyes.

"You think I'm unstable because of what happened when I was a kid."

"I think that," Drew said, choosing his words carefully, "you're very good at telling stories."

"You think I made all this up."

"I didn't say that either."

"Or maybe you think I'm imagining things, and that if you leave now and don't hear any more, it will be like none of this ever happened . . . that you'll be safe . . . but you won't."

Drew's jaw tightened despite his fear. "Is that a threat?"

"No," Logan said simply. "Just the truth."

Drew looked into Logan's eyes—it was nearly impossible to look away from them—searching for a sign that Logan was playing him, baiting him to continue with the "scene," like he'd done in the bedroom a few weeks ago. But this time there was no teasing glint, no playful wink, not even the ghost of a smile at the corner of his mouth. Either Logan was completely serious, or he was a far better actor than Drew had initially given him credit for. Either way, it didn't really matter. Drew had heard enough, and now he wanted to leave.

But still, the fear held him frozen in place while the memory of Coach's warning on the soccer pitch last week echoed back to him: *Steer clear of that kid, Thor.*

"I have to get home," Drew said. "My brother's gonna be waiting up for me."

Logan knew that Drew lived with his brother, Jason. He knew that Jason was seven years older than Drew and that he had become Drew's legal guardian three years ago after their mother had committed herself to a psychiatric hospital for severe depression. He knew that Drew's father had died in a car accident when Drew was still a toddler and that Drew's mother had never fully recovered from this tragedy. He knew that the Thor brothers had moved here last spring because Jason got a job offer that paid double what he'd been making in California. Logan had been very thorough in his research. He knew that Jason traveled quite a bit for his work, often leaving Drew on his own for days at a time. And he knew that this weekend—the upcoming Halloween weekend—would be one of those times Drew would be all alone in the house.

In his mind, Logan could see the three boys standing at the top of the stairs. Watching. Waiting.

He shook off the image.

Not this time, he thought.

He looked at Drew again, and what he saw made him ache in a place he'd thought long dead. Drew and he were both seventeen—the same age Martyn had been on that fateful Halloween night seven years ago. But right now, Drew looked younger and, despite his physical stature, infinitely more vulnerable, like an apprehensive boy anxious to be excused from the table.

Logan nodded and looked down at his coffee cup, which was nearly empty now. Drew took this as a sign that they were done and got up. He put on his jacket and was ready to go, but when he looked down at Logan, something tugged at him from inside. The fear he'd felt only moments ago had receded—Logan wasn't quite as spooky when he wasn't looking you straight in the eye—and the anger from before resurfaced, along with all the messy feelings attached to that night he'd spent with the boy, L.

Not the "imprint" of Logan but the *actor* Logan had hired to play the part of L, Drew reminded himself bitterly. An innocent little kid who could have been seriously injured or killed that night. And for what? A scene? Drew couldn't help feeling sorry for everything that Logan had gone through as a kid—no kid should have to live through a nightmare like that. But still, it didn't excuse what Logan had put him through. He knew that he should just walk out and not look back, but some part of him couldn't let it go without taking one last stab.

"Why me?" Drew asked, working to keep his anger in check. "Of all the guys you could have picked to play out this little scene with, why me?"

Logan remained silent for a moment, then said softly, "I didn't pick you. She did."

"Right, the ghost of your dead babysitter," Drew said, shaking his head in wonder at Logan's tenacity. He still wanted to go, but he couldn't resist asking one more question, even though he already knew the answer would likely be more of the same nonsense. "And why did she pick me? What's so special about me?"

Logan looked up at him in genuine confusion. He'd assumed that Drew had already put the pieces together. It had never occurred to him that Drew might have overlooked this vital piece of information during his recent online research into the deaths of Marilyn and Martyn. It was such a glaringly obvious detail that he'd felt sure Drew would have easily discovered it. But by the look on his face, it was clear that Drew was in the dark.

"You really don't know, do you?" Logan said.

With those cool grey eyes upon him again, Drew felt the fear creeping back in. He pushed against it and forced himself to ask, "Know what?"

Logan held him in his gaze for a moment longer and then said, "You're living in the house where it happened. Marilyn's house. Your presence there has awakened her."

Drew froze while his mind raced forward: *He's lying. It's just another twist in his sick little scene. He's trying to get inside your head and scare you. Don't let him in.*

"You must have felt her by now," Logan said calmly. "Particularly over the past month. She'll only get stronger as her night approaches. She'll come to you in dreams—or what you believe to be dreams. Each time she'll get a little closer, and by Halloween night she'll reach her apex . . . and step out of the dream."

Drew stared at Logan for a long, uncertain moment. Then he swallowed bitterly and shook his head. "You're good," he said. "You've got the act down perfect. But I'm not buying it this time . . . I'm not . . . " He stopped and looked away, and a genuine sadness touched his eyes. "You know, I actually liked you. In spite of everything I'd heard about you before that day you approached me to help you with your scene, I thought you were cool, and I wanted to be your friend." He swallowed again, his Adam's apple moving as if in slow motion, and with effort, he said: "I don't think we should see each other anymore."

A long silence followed, and in it, the two of them looked like figures frozen in tableau—Drew staring down at the floor; Logan staring down at his coffee cup—waiting for the curtain to fall. But this wasn't a scene, and neither of them was acting.

With a suddenness that surprised even him, Drew broke his pose and left the coffee shop.

B ut it didn't end there.

Several hours later, after the sun had gone down and the nearly full moon had risen in the dark sky, Logan sat in his car and gazed at the house across the street. Though it was currently occupied by the Thor brothers, it was still Marilyn's house, and always would be. He was parked under the canopy of a great willow, his eyes focused on the wide picture window, which offered a full view of the living room. With the curtains pulled back, the living room resembled a stage . . . where the action played out nightly between the two characters who resided within.

Only this wasn't a scene in a play, and Drew and Jason Thor weren't actors. Logan had been reminding himself of this fact ever since he'd first started parking here across the street from his former sitter's house. That had been a little over three weeks ago, at the beginning of October, when he'd first sensed Marilyn's essence in the air.

It had come unexpectedly at school, in the hallway between classes. He had been walking along, thinking of nothing in particular, when suddenly he'd caught her "scent," the way one catches a whiff of perfume when a lady passes by. A delicate aroma, scarcely detectable, and yet it had invaded his senses like a potent drug. When he'd turned to seek out the source, his sight zoomed in on an unlikely subject. At the time, he hadn't even known Drew's name. He only knew that Drew was the new guy all the girls were drooling over.

Logan hadn't approached him immediately. He'd

waited until school let out and followed Drew home at a safe distance. It had become clear to Logan where Drew was headed well before the weathered blue Mustang pulled into the driveway of Marilyn's old house. Logan had gone back that very night, parked across the street in what would become his usual spot, and viewed the action beyond the picture window until the lights had gone out. He did the same thing the following night and several nights after. Each time, he sat patiently in his car under the shadow of the willow, watching and waiting.

His patience was rewarded on the fifth night. As usual, nothing out of the ordinary had happened. The brothers went about their nightly routine. Dinner at six. Homework at the dining room table for Drew until seven or eight. Then the two of them would watch TV in the living room, Drew sprawled out on the sofa while Jason lay back in the recliner. And finally, around eleven or so, they would head up to bed.

But on this particular night, something different had occurred. Just before the last light went out—the dim light at the foot of the stairwell—something flashed at the far corner of the darkened picture window. A luminescent image that had yet to reach solid form. It had come and gone so quickly that, had Logan blinked, he might have missed it.

But he hadn't blinked.

He had seen the lovely girl in that darkened pane of glass. She had been standing in the corner of the living room, gazing up toward the stairs that the two brothers had just ascended. And though she had not seen Logan in his car across the street, *he* had clearly seen *her*. And judging by the look in her eyes, he was fairly certain what it was that she wanted from one or both of the brothers who'd just headed up the stairs for bed.

He had waited a few days before approaching Drew in the student parking lot after school. By then, he'd come up with the plan to ease Drew into his confidence. The scene, which had more or less worked before, back when he was a kid, seemed the best way to achieve his goal of winning Drew's trust.

But of course, Logan thought as he sat in his car now, gazing through the window across the street, *that was before L had come into the picture.*

This was true. L had indeed changed the . . . complexion of things. There had been many pitfalls and perils to consider before setting the plan into motion, but the imprint of his younger self—so very like Logan in many ways, and yet discrete—had not been one of them. Logan had never once considered the possibility that L might be "awakened" by the very thing that had drawn Logan to Drew in the first place.

Marilyn's essence.

But in hindsight, it made perfect sense: with Drew inside Logan's house, and Marilyn's "scent" upon him, it would have only been a matter of time before L would rise and become more . . . cohesive. And L was sharp—nearly as sharp as Logan was now—and possessed of all the willful fortitude of a child. Logan could not imagine a greater adversary he could possibly face than his ten-year-old self.

And yet the question begged: was L truly at cross purposes with Logan? Had it been his intention to cause the rift between Drew and Logan, or had the clever little imprint merely been trying to help out with the plan?

Or had he simply been looking for attention and, in Drew, discovered precisely the right guy to get that attention from?

The little guy had certainly put Drew through the paces that night at the amusement park—precisely the sort of thing Logan would have done with Martyn to get his attention. Though Drew and Martyn were not alike physically, they did share a similar mindset. Both ruled by a strong sense of responsibility and compassion, with open hearts worn so carelessly on their sleeves. It could be that L had simply gravitated to Drew as a surrogate big brother.

But he'd felt safer with Drew than he ever had with Martyn, Logan thought. I *had felt safer,* he amended.

He recalled the way L had curled up close, nestling his cheek against Drew's shoulder as Drew carried him up to his old childhood room . . . the way he'd clung to Drew when Drew tried to set him on the bed, and the way he'd relaxed when Drew rubbed his back gently.

Logan tried to remember if Martyn had ever shown him that sort of affection, but it was difficult to see through the haze in his mind, where things were rapidly getting more and more confusing. And suddenly, he found himself wondering the *real* reason L had felt safe that night at the amusement park. Could L have drawn close to the handsome jock for another reason? Possibly the faint yet intoxicating essence of *Marilyn* coming off of Drew? But if so, why had L gone to such lengths to *warn* Drew about Marilyn?

And the oldest of the three imaginary boys, a voice within reminded him. *L had warned Drew about that as well.*

It was true. L had spilled that messy little can of worms as well.

. . . you needn't fear the younger ones . . . but the oldest boy is dangerous . . . you have to stay away from him . . .

As Logan recalled the moment when L had passed this warning along to Drew, a wave of experimental tendrils ascended his spine and radiated over every inch of his body as a more distant memory resurfaced . . .

It had been Marilyn who'd told him about the three imaginary boys.

He had woken from a bad dream one chilly October night. The naked branches of the tree outside his window cast long and deciduous shadows against the walls of his bedroom, like spindly claws reaching for purchase. As he lay in his bed, he could hear Marilyn and Martyn in the next room, the soft sounds of their intimacy. When he called out to her, she came at once, and as she held him close and stroked his hair, she told him that everything was all right.

Normally, this would have soothed him, but on that night, his body remained rigid. He'd seen the three boys standing on the lawn outside his window and could not erase the image from his mind. They had looked exactly as they would some seven years later in the mouth of the tunnel at the foot of the Hell-e-vator. All three of them stood in a row, with their faces painted white and their eyes shining silver. Waiting and watching. A frightening triad of spectres.

But when he told Marilyn about the boys, she didn't seem frightened at all. In fact, she smiled, as if she knew all about them. And she did. She said he had nothing to fear from the boys, that they were only imaginary, like the boys in the song, *Three Imaginary Boys*.

Logan knew the song well. It was one of Marilyn's favorites, and she played it all the time. It was sort of spooky, and he didn't understand all of the lyrics, but it was a good song, and since Marilyn loved it, he loved it too.

As she held him in her arms, she told him precisely who the three imaginary boys were.

"They are *you*, my angel," she said softly. "They represent the phases of your life—the boy you were, the boy you are, and the boy you will one day be. And their sole purpose is to watch over you and guide you to your destiny. They only want what's best for you, and they would never harm you. They're your special guardians."

Logan had believed her at the time, but now he wasn't so sure. And judging by what had happened last Friday at the amusement park, it appeared L was convinced that at least one of the imaginary boys posed a very real danger. The oldest of the three—the one who, as Marilyn had put it, was the boy that Logan would one day become.

Was it possible that day had arrived? Could L's appearance have been triggered by his belief that Logan posed a threat to Drew? Was it possible that some secret darkness within Logan could have stirred the slumbering imprint of his ten-year-old self into action? Was it even possible for an imprint to actively engage in a preemptive maneuver against its future self?

Logan thought about this as he sat in his car, gazing at the house across the street. While it made perfect sense that L's thoughts and feelings would extend forward into Logan's memory, the notion that Logan's secret desires—whether conscious or subconscious—could somehow make their way back in time to L seemed highly improbable.

Improbable, but not impossible, the voice within whispered.

But even so, Logan countered. *We both want the same thing, L and I. We both want to protect Drew.*

Logan waited, but the voice within offered nothing more.

Logan thought, *I can save him . . . I* will *save him.*

It was a willful sentiment, delivered with the conviction of a young boy determined to prove his resolve.

The voice within chuckled like a teenager challenging his kid brother: *And how do you intend to do that?*

Logan didn't have to think about it. There was only one thing he could do.

He had to get Drew out of Marilyn's house on Halloween night. Her special night. Her anniversary. The one night of the year that the dead are free to roam and do precisely as they please.

Logan turned away from the window and closed his eyes, and shortly, he began to drift . . . and dream . . .

In his dream, Logan was at Terror Fest, sitting in one of the suspended seats of the Hell-e-vator, and Drew was strapping him in. Logan could hear his own voice saying, *Are you apprehensive?* Only it didn't sound like his seventeen-year-old voice; it sounded like the voice of L. That's when he realized he was back in his ten-year-old body. Then Drew was in the seat next to him, and as the ascent of the ride began, Logan could see the three boys in the mouth of the tunnel, all gazing upward with shining silver eyes. Only this time, they were not alone. Marilyn was with them, watching and waiting. It wasn't until the ride reached the top that the cold hand of fear gripped Logan's heart . . . because he knew that the three boys and Marilyn would be waiting for him at the bottom.

When the drop finally came, instead of reaching the safety of the ground, he and Drew were both sent plummeting toward the Silver Bullet roller coaster. They landed with a dreamlike thud—Logan on the tracks, Drew on the maintenance platform. Just as it was that night almost two weeks ago.

Only this time, something truly horrifying occurred.

When Drew reached out to him and took his hand, Logan did not allow himself to be pulled to safety. Instead, he pulled Drew onto the tracks and held him close. And as the train of cars came barreling around the wide curve, headed straight for them, Logan shouted, *It's the only way out! It's the only way we can cheat her! She's here! She's here!*

At the moment of impact, they were separated again. Both of them fell with tremendous velocity toward the house with the wide picture window on the dark street, but before either made contact with the roof, Logan woke with a start.

He sat behind the wheel of his car, disoriented for a moment. A sheen of cold sweat had broken out across his brow. He took a quick gasping breath, then looked at the dashboard clock. It was a few minutes after midnight—a full hour after the Thor brothers' usual bedtime. But when he looked at the house across the street, an eerie glow illuminated the living room. The lights were out, but the TV was still on. It flickered against the lone figure in the room.

Drew lay in his usual spot on the sofa, dressed in jeans and a T-shirt. His head was propped up on a cushion against one armrest, his bare feet extended over the edge of the other armrest. One arm dangled off the open side of the sofa, the knuckles resting on the floor; the other extended above his head, the limp hand touching his hair.

At a glance, Logan could tell that Drew was sleeping. But it took a moment for him to grasp that Drew was dreaming . . . or at least *appeared* to be dreaming.

Logan watched as Drew's body twitched and shifted in a hypnotic sleep-dance—subtle, almost graceful movements, as if Drew were reacting to an external stimulus . . . as if a pair of invisible hands were moving over his body, teasing, tantalizing, coaxing . . .

Then suddenly there was an unexpected movement. The hem of Drew's T-shirt began to rise on its own, exposing his abdomen, then his chest. Still sleeping, Drew arched his back to facilitate the removal of his shirt, which fell to the carpet in a floating manner. Now he lay with both arms stretched on the armrest above his head, and his body began to move more rhythmically. His chest swelled, his arms tensed, his lips parted, his nostrils flared.

Logan sat in his car across the street, frozen. Through the window now, Drew's sleeping body shifted again—this time to facilitate the removal of his jeans, which slid off his hips and down his legs in a dreamlike motion. The jeans fell to the carpet beside the T-shirt. Drew lay stretched out on the sofa, clad only in his boxers now. His exposed body appeared to shimmer in the flickering light of the TV.

Logan wanted to look away, but he couldn't. In spite of everything he knew, everything he'd experienced, some part of his mind screamed out, *This isn't real, this can't be real! It's just a trick. I'm still dreaming.*

But the other part of his mind—the part that knew the

truth—understood all too well that it was not a trick. He was not dreaming. This was real.

He watched as one invisible hand moved inside Drew's boxers and the other pressed against Drew's bare chest. He watched as Drew's back arched and his hips thrust upward into that invisible grasp. He watched as Drew writhed and gasped in ecstasy. He watched in deathly silence as the scene played out on the other side of the window, and a raw passion burned from deep within.

At the point of climax, Logan felt as if he might actually pass out. Despite the chilly breeze passing through the open window of his car, his body was bathed in sweat, and his heart was racing wildly. In that final moment—when Drew's hands clutched the sofa's armrest and his body tensed with multiple spasms of ecstasy—a wave of revulsion rose from within, threatening to consume Logan whole. But what happened next brought Logan back from the brink and thrust him into full consciousness.

As Drew's body relaxed and eased back into the cushions of the sofa, *she* rose from within. Not as a mere flicker at the corner of the darkened window, as she had appeared on that night several weeks ago, but not fully cohesive either. Not yet, anyway.

She rose from inside of Drew, like a semitransparent image, and stepped onto the floor with balletic grace. Her naked body, deliciously milky and supple, shimmered with an ethereal glow. Her gaze fell upon the sleeping figure of Drew, the passion still burning in her eyes.

Then, in a sudden yet graceful movement, her head pivoted toward the front window, and her ever-changing eyes went dark as she spotted the car across the street.

My sweet boy, she whispered, without parting her lips.

Then she floated fast to the picture window and gazed out at Logan with huge sparkling eyes.

In the car, Logan reared back in horror. But he could not tear his eyes from her. She was as beautiful in death as she had been in life, and, like his older brother Martyn, he had never been able to resist her.

As they stared at one another, the soft sound of the music pouring from the car's speakers invaded Logan's ears—Lifehouse's *Just Another Name*. The same song that the zombie band had sung at Terror Fest the night that Drew and L had gone to the amusement park. Only now the lyrics held much more meaning . . .

Which mask will you wear today?
How 'bout the one with the pretty smile?
To you it's just another day
In a life you haven't lived in quite a while . . .

Logan's eyes darkened as those lyrics burned into his consciousness, but the fear still lingered behind his steely gaze. He wasn't sure how long the eye lock between him and the ghost of his former sitter had lasted—it seemed like an eternity—but by the time she'd begun to fade, it didn't really matter.

What *did* matter was that Logan had been right about her return. She was real. She'd come back to her old house, the place where she'd died. Perhaps, she'd never left.

But even more important, *Drew* had seen her . . . and not just in his most recent dream. At some point during the protracted staring match between Logan and Marilyn, Drew must have woken and seen her at the window because he was sitting up on the sofa now, with a look of pure terror in his eyes.

When those terror-stricken eyes darted to the front window and saw the Porsche across the street, Logan offered a scarcely perceptible nod, as if to say *Welcome to my nightmare*. But despite his hard gaze, he was trembling just as fiercely as Drew.

They didn't come into contact again until after the final school bell on the following day.

Drew had stayed awake most of the night and only got a few hours of restless sleep when he finally dozed off sometime after four AM. And even then, it had been impossible to get the image of the naked girl out of his mind. He did not dream of her again—at least not in the manner he had earlier that evening. But she was there on the periphery of his thoughts, lurking in the shadows of his subconscious, biding her time, waiting for her special night to arrive. The night she died. Halloween.

The one night of the year that the dead are free to roam and do precisely as they please.

Drew couldn't remember where he'd heard that statement before, but he believed it. As crazy as it seemed, he now believed that the dead could rise on Halloween.

The image of Logan's deceased babysitter standing at the front window in his living room—the dream of her rising from within him—had changed everything.

Logan was clever, and Drew could see how a clever guy with unlimited financial resources could arrange an elaborate scenario like what had happened at the amusement park with L and the two girls—Marilyn and Danae—that would only require hiring look-alike actors to play out a scene. But what had happened last night—the vivid dream from which he awoke to find the glowing spectre of a naked dead girl standing right inside his living room; a girl who then faded out of existence right before Drew's wide staring eyes—that was not something Logan could have arranged.

She was inside me. I could feel her touching and probing inside *me.*

He thought about this as he stood at the touchline of the soccer pitch, gazing out at the lone figure on the center circle. He pushed back on the thought with effort as he crossed the brittle grass. He stopped a few paces behind Logan and waited a moment before speaking.

"What does she want from me?"

It came out harsher than he'd intended, but Logan didn't seem to notice. He just continued to gaze out at the steely October sky in silence. A sudden breeze riffled his shiny, dark hair. Drew waited.

"They used to come here at night," Logan said, still looking off to the sky. "Martyn was on the soccer team, and she would come to watch him play, and after dark, they would return. They would lie on this very spot and gaze at the stars. She told me about it. She said they would curl up for hours and sometimes even fall asleep in each other's arms beneath the stars. She said she felt like she could climb inside him and stay there forever."

Drew felt a shiver as he recalled the sensation of her touch from within. It had both repelled and excited him at once. He felt the urge to tell Logan about this, but kept quiet. Even though he no longer believed that Logan had lied to him—at least not about ghosts and imprints—some part of Drew still didn't trust Logan. Not completely, anyway. He couldn't get over the feeling that, despite all the information Logan had given him, there was still something the guy was holding back. Some critical piece of the puzzle that, once in place, would bring the entire picture into focus.

Also, Drew had not forgotten that Logan had admitted to killing Marilyn. He understood that there had been extenuating circumstances, that Logan had just been a kid at the time, and that Marilyn had used her power to instigate that act of unspeakable violence. But still, he could not bring himself to dismiss the fact that it was Logan who'd wielded the knife that had set all of this madness into motion. It didn't matter if Logan hadn't *intended* to kill her; what mattered was that he *did* kill her. And now she was back.

And Drew was certain of one thing: Logan knew exactly what Marilyn was after.

He latched onto this thought with singular purpose and used it to push back against the fear within. "Why did she come to me? What does she want?"

"She wants revenge," Logan said softly.

"Revenge against who? I haven't done anything to her. Why doesn't she just come after you? I mean, no offense, but you're the one who killed her."

Logan didn't look offended. He just shook his head with a bitter half-smile. "You still don't get it. This isn't about *you*. You're not the star of this scene. You're not even a supporting player. You're just a prop—the gun that shows up in the first act so the leading lady can use it in the third act. A simple yet effective means to an end. No offense."

Drew was surprised at how deeply Logan's condescending quips could still cut, but he refused to take the bait. Instead, he held his tongue and waited for Logan to get to the point. When Logan spoke again, there was no trace of the condescending tone in his voice.

"She doesn't want to *get* you," he said. "She wants to *be* you." He turned to look at Drew now. "Last night wasn't the first time you've seen her in your dreams, was it?"

Drew shook his head slowly.

"How long has she been coming to you? A few weeks? A month?"

"A couple of weeks."

Logan gave him a short, bitter smile, and Drew suddenly looked defensive.

"I didn't even know who she was until you spilled your guts at the coffee shop—and even then, I didn't put it all together until I saw her last night. I thought I was just having dreams about some random girl. I couldn't even remember her face."

Logan shook his head dismissively. "And over these past few weeks, have you noticed anything out of place at your house? A book you left on your desk before you went to bed, and then when you woke up the next morning it was back on the shelf with your other books; a full glass of water on your night table that was empty in the morning, even though you have no memory of waking and drinking it in the night—anything unusual like that?"

Drew nodded, with a measure of caution.

"Been feeling more sluggish when you wake, as if you didn't get enough sleep, even when you've gone to bed early?"

Drew didn't respond this time, but a prickling sensation rose at the nape of his neck.

Logan shook his head with a soundless sigh. "I had an idea, but I wasn't sure until last night . . . until what I'd seen in your living room through the window . . . "

He looked off to the sky again. It would be getting dark soon, and he didn't want to be here after nightfall—not on the same spot Marilyn had lain with his brother, and the memory of their intimacy still lingered. So he forced himself to go on.

"You felt her inside of you, didn't you." It wasn't a question, and Logan didn't wait for a response. "I saw her . . . I saw her rise from your body. I saw her inside you, and it was like . . . it was like she was trying you on, like a coat or a new pair of shoes. Breaking you in, so to speak. And if what you say is true, if she's been coming to you in your dreams for a few weeks now, then she's had a good deal of practice. From what I saw last night, it would appear she's getting good at it. Good enough that pretty soon she won't need you in there anymore. She'll be able to do it all on her own." Logan paused and looked at Drew, whose face seemed suddenly pale. "Are you starting to get the point?"

Drew swallowed back his fear and said, "But why does she need me. Why doesn't she just come after you?"

"Contrary to popular belief, spirits of the dead can't harm the living. They can haunt you, play tricks on you, even drive you insane enough to harm yourself. But to pose a *physical* threat, a spirit needs a living vessel . . . one with whom it shares an intimate bond."

"I don't even *know* her," Drew snapped, but it came out more fearful than forceful.

"But *she* knows *you*," Logan said calmly. "Or more accurately, she knows the *essence* of you. The same essence that Martyn possessed. You're the good guy in this scene. The hero—at least to her, you are. And in the end, the hero always takes down the bad guy . . . and if you haven't already guessed it, the 'bad guy' is me. And in order to exact revenge on me, she needs a warm body to occupy." A mournful smile touched Logan's lips, but his eyes shone dark and hard.

Drew shook his head. "It doesn't make sense. I've seen the two of them, Marilyn and her friend Danae, twice now—first at a swim meet in New Lennox, and again at the amusement park that night with L—and they didn't look like Marilyn did last night. They weren't glowing. They were *real*. That Danae girl *touched* me."

"And how did it feel when she touched you? Was her hand warm?"

"It was a cold night," Drew protested. "You know that. You were there—or at least your imprint was—you have to remember it." A sudden hopeful thought occurred to Drew, and he lunged at it with fervent desperation. "And what about my phone? That girl Danae—she took my phone and put her number in it. How could she do that without a whatchacallit . . . a vessel?"

Logan surprised Drew by nodding in agreement. "You're right," he said. "Call her."

Drew froze; his eyes narrowed in confusion.

"Take out your phone and call her right now."

Drew fished his phone out of his pocket and scrolled through his list of contacts, but there was no number for Danae. He scrolled down to the "M"s to see if maybe she'd given him Marilyn's number, but there was nothing there either. He went up and down the list of numbers a few more times, just to be certain, but found no number for either of the girls he'd met at Terror Fest that night. When he looked up from his phone, Logan was gazing at him with an empathetic expression.

"They're very good at playing tricks on the living," Logan said softly.

And that's when the look of fear returned to Drew's eyes.

They sat in Logan's car, both of them staring through the windscreen as the sun went down. Neither of them had spoken since they left the soccer pitch. It was Drew who broke the silence.

"What happens once she . . . takes control? What happens to me? Will I still be . . . will I still be inside my body . . . or will I just . . . you know . . . ?"

Logan remained silent for a moment longer. Then he said softly, "You'll most likely have been expelled by then."

Now it was Drew's turn to be silent before speaking. "And then what happens?"

"Then she comes after me," Logan said simply.

"And that's it? That's how it ends? I get 'expelled'—which I'm assuming is more permanent than it sounds—and you get knifed by me . . . or by her wearing my body, in which case everyone, including my brother, will think I went nuts and killed you."

"Not necessarily," Logan said pensively. "She could dispose of my body after. She's a very resourceful girl."

"Yeah, great—so what, she just goes on living in my body for as long as it lasts her?" Drew shook his head in disbelief. "Tell me that this is the part where you say, 'No worries, I have this great plan.' Because I'm really starting to freak out here, man."

Logan looked at Drew's trembling hands and said, "Actually, I do have a plan."

"Great. Let's hear it."

"I'm not sure you're going to like it."

"If it involves keeping your psycho dead babysitter out of my body, I'm all for it."

"It involves L," Logan said flatly.

Drew's body tensed, and his eyes suddenly looked cautious.

"Marilyn always had a soft spot for L," Logan continued in a measured tone. "He was her one weakness—her Achilles heel, so to speak. If we could convince L to . . . call out to her, there's a good chance she'd come to him . . . *if* she felt that he was in genuine distress or danger . . . "

"I don't get it," Drew said, shaking his head. "How would getting L to call to her solve anything? And why would she come to L after what he did to her? Isn't that the whole reason why she's back, to get even with L for killing her?"

Logan said, "She doesn't want to hurt L. She would never consciously harm a child. She wants to take revenge on *me*."

"But L *is* you, or at least he was you when you were a kid. And that's when you killed her, right? When you were a kid. When you were still L, right?"

Logan shook his head gently. "It doesn't work that way when you're dealing with entities that exist in parallel universes."

"Well, then I'm totally lost, so you'd better explain how it *does* work, and fast because I'm about *this* close to losing my fucking mind here."

Drew pressed his fists against his legs to keep them from shaking while Logan collected his thoughts.

"Once we move on to a new stage in our lives," Logan began, choosing his words carefully, "we sever the cord that connects us to our childhood. While we retain some memories, others fade. And sometimes we acquire 'new memories'—ones we cannot account for, because they are not from our actual experiences as a child. Some people think of these new memories as *déjà vu* when in fact they're just the memories that our imprints are forwarding to us from the experiences they continue to have in the parallel universes where they live—the same way that L's experiences that night with you were forwarded into my memory."

Drew still looked dubious. "But if the connection between the two of you was severed once you left your childhood behind, how could L's experiences be passed on to your memory?"

Logan offered a small smile as if to say *touché*. "Think of it like a receiver. Or a beacon in space. Even though light-years may separate the beacon from its origin, the signal continues to come through." He paused as if debating whether to elaborate on the point, and then said, "In some cases—not many, but some—certain gifted individuals have managed to *transmit* as well as receive."

A wave of goosebumps raced over Drew's arms. "You're saying that you could contact L and ask him to help us."

"Not exactly. It's not like a phone line or email. It's a little more . . . complicated."

Drew's eyes narrowed, and his heart began to beat a little faster. Logan held him in his gaze.

"What I *could* do," Logan said, carefully, "is attempt to place a notion in L's mind. Not much different than the memories he's forwarded to me. Same principle, only a bit more potent and persuasive. Because he doesn't possess my knowledge of current events, it won't come to him as a memory. It will be more like his own idea, like the voice of his conscience—or his better angels, if you will—whispering into his ear."

Drew uttered a short, humorless laugh. "Like inception."

Logan's brow furrowed.

"Like the movie *Inception*. You plant the idea in his mind, and he believes it's his own."

Logan nodded. "Something like that."

The muscles in Drew's jaw tensed. "And once this idea is in his head, he'll call to Marilyn, and she'll come to him."

Logan nodded.

"And then what happens?"

"Then," Logan said calmly, "he'll take her with him."

"Back to his parallel universe."

Logan nodded again.

"And what then?"

Logan drew an even breath. "And then she'll be trapped there."

"Trapped how?"

"She's a spirit," Logan said with a sharp glint in his eye. "A dark spirit. And as legend has it, dark spirits can only travel in a straight line—unless they are accompanied by an entity pure of soul . . . an innocent."

"Like L," Drew said.

"Like L," Logan agreed. "Of course, I'd have to make sure to provide him with a winding route, with lots of twists and turns back to his universe, but that shouldn't be too difficult. The kid loves puzzles and mazes."

Drew sat in silence, thinking about it. Then he shook his head as if something was missing, something that Logan wasn't telling him. "It sounds like a plan," he said, "using an imaginary kid to trap a ghost in an imaginary universe, but—"

He stopped and looked into Logan's eyes. Logan did not insult him by looking away. Drew's mouth curled into a snarl of disgust as the truth came slamming home like a gut punch.

"It's not an imaginary universe, is it."

"I never implied that it was," Logan said.

"No, but if I hadn't said anything, you'd have let me go on believing it was, wouldn't you?" Drew expelled an angry breath through his nostrils. "And L—you'd have let me believe that he was imaginary, too. Just an imprint of your childhood. But he's much more than that, isn't he? He's a real kid. Just as real as you and me. And in that universe where he lives, he can grow up to be anyone he wants to be. He doesn't have to be you. His life doesn't have to come to this crap. He can make his own path. And that scares the shit out of you, doesn't it?"

Logan remained silent, but still he did not avert his gaze. Drew snorted a bitter laugh.

"Man, you are some piece of work. You set up your little scenes and move the players around like chess pieces to serve your own purposes. It doesn't matter that they're real people with real feelings. To you, it's all just a play or a movie, right? And screw anybody who gets in your way. Is that about it?"

Logan's countenance remained cool, detached. Drew looked off to the dark sky and released a heavy sigh.

"And you suckered me right into this thing and put me behind the eight ball."

"I didn't do anything to you," Logan said softly. "*She* came to you because you moved into her house. I only intervened to save you—"

"By offering up an innocent kid to be sacrificed. Yeah, you're a real hero."

Logan's eye twitched. "That innocent kid is the one who wielded the knife."

Drew shot a hard glare at Logan. "That innocent kid used to be you. And you said yourself that he was coerced into doing it."

Logan could not deny this.

"And not to put a damper on your fire," Drew went on, "but if your brilliant little plan of trapping your babysitter from hell in another universe actually could succeed, wouldn't that just end up putting *you* behind the eight ball? I mean, if she kills L, wouldn't that make you cease to exist in the here and now?"

"She won't be able to kill him," Logan said, "because, in order to kill him, she would need a body . . . and since the only compatible body is yours, once we trap her in L's universe, she won't have access to you—which is the point of my 'brilliant plan' to begin with." He paused and shifted gears. "She would never kill a child, anyway, least of all L. Like I said, it's *me* she's after. And by taking her revenge on me, she can have her cake and eat it too."

Drew looked lost. Logan elaborated.

"Like you said, if she were to kill L, I would very likely cease to exist. Mission accomplished. *But* by bypassing L and going straight for me, she can have her revenge on the one who killed her without harming a single hair on the head of the innocent child. Indeed, L will continue to live happily and safely in his own universe, completely unaware of the messy end that his future self has come to in *this* universe. Twisted but logical, when you think about it."

Drew could see what Logan was getting at, but still something gnawed at him. "So, if we trap her in L's universe before she can use me to get to you, what happens with her and L? She doesn't have a 'vessel,' so she can't kill him—I get that. But I take it she's still pissed because she couldn't get you. So what happens with her and L?"

Logan paused, then said, "She'll most likely pick up with him pretty much where she left off."

"Poisoning his mind like she did before."

"He's a tough little kid. There's nothing she could throw at him that he couldn't handle. Trust me, I know."

Drew's eyes burned with genuine loathing. "He's not you. He's nothing like you."

Logan said simply, "He's me before there was a me."

Drew shook his head. "No. He's different."

"How so?"

Drew hesitated. In his mind, he could see himself carrying the sleeping boy up to his room after their long night at the amusement park. He could hear the boy's voice calling to him softly from the bed where he lay tucked safely under the covers . . .

You are my brave and loyal knight, and I know now that

you would risk your life to defend me. I know that you're not my brother . . . but you should have been. Had it been so, things would be different.

Recalling those words, the unmistakable sincerity in the boy's voice when he'd spoken them, Drew answered Logan's question without further hesitation. "He's different from you because there's still hope for him."

F or a long while, they sat in silence.

Logan wasn't surprised that Drew had chosen L's safety over his own—indeed, he had *counted* on it. Sending Marilyn's spirit off to L's universe had never been his intention anyway—the last thing Logan wanted or needed at this stage of the game was that cunning little viper in a position to whisper sweet nothings into L's impressionable ear. But what Logan hadn't expected was the extent of Drew's distaste for the plan, and further, Drew's feelings of complete contempt toward Logan for even *thinking* of such a plan. Nor had he expected the depth of the bond that Drew had formed with L. He had simply assumed that Drew's innate chivalry would conquer the natural instinct for self-preservation. And it had. At this very moment, Drew was just as willing to place himself in danger as he had been that night at the amusement park when L had stepped out onto the tracks of the roller coaster.

But this is different, Logan thought. Back at the park, there hadn't been any time to think. Drew had simply responded to the imminent threat to L, the same as anyone would respond to a child in danger. But in the present situation, Drew had more than enough time to think, and after thinking long and hard, he was consciously *choosing* to protect L.

Logan felt a primal stirring from deep within. The irony was almost unbearably profound: a guy who so clearly loathed him in the here and now was willing to make the ultimate sacrifice to protect the child that he, Logan, used to be. Logan thought of Martyn, his older brother, the one who should have been there to protect him when he was just a kid. Had Martyn possessed even *half* of Drew's inner strength, things would have been very different, Logan was certain of this.

I think we have company.

It was Danae who'd said that. She'd giggled, but it had been a nervous giggle, and she'd pulled the sheet up to cover her breasts. Marilyn had smiled and called out to him, but Logan had just stood there at the bedroom door, staring at the three of them in his brother's bed. Martyn in between the two girls. All of them naked, touching each other, kissing each other's private areas. Then Martyn had looked up with a drunken smile, one hand still on Marilyn's breast.

It's OK, he'd said to the girls. *He's just curious.* Then to Logan: *It's OK, L. We're just having a party. Come 'ere, little buddy. It's all right. This is Danae, and you know Marilyn. It's OK. They won't bite you. Come 'ere.*

As much as he'd wanted to turn away, run back to his room, and bury himself under the covers, Logan had not been able to resist the gentle sound of his brother's voice.

The memory came at him now in a flood of images and sensations: the smell of beer on Martyn's breath, both nostalgic and repellent at once; Martyn taking his small hand and placing it on Marilyn's bare breast; the sound of his own heart beating so wildly that he'd been almost certain he would faint; his eyes drifting to the little black box lying on the bed between Martyn and Marilyn; the drunken smile curling at the corners of Martyn's mouth.

Do you want to push the button?

He'd nodded as if in a dream, and Martyn had laughed.

Go ahead, Martyn had said, *push it.*

With one hand still on Marilyn's breast, Logan had reached out with the other and pressed the tiny button on the black box. It beeped as it sent a dose of insulin through the fine tubing that trailed to the pad affixed to his older brother's stomach, and, with a smile of delight, Martyn ruffled his hair.

From that distant place in his memory, Logan could hear Danae asking, *How old is he? . . .* and Martyn's response: *He's gotta learn sometime . . .* and then the sound of drunken laughter following him all the way down that black hole he'd fallen into, just like the rabbit-hole in the story Marilyn had read to him earlier that same evening.

Logan's gaze remained fixed on the crisp night sky as the memory faded. He waited until it was completely gone before breaking the silence. "There's only one other option," he said.

Drew was still angry, but he hadn't left the car. "What?" he said, stiffly.

"We remove you from the equation."

Drew turned to him, with no attempt to conceal the suspicion in his eyes. "Remove me how?"

"Relax. It's not as dramatic as it sounds. We only need to remove you from your house on Halloween." Drew's eyes were still narrowed in suspicion, but Logan could see that he was already getting it. "If you're not in your house on Halloween, then she won't be able to get to you."

Drew thought about this, then said, "But she got to me at the amusement park, and the swim meet in New Lennox—"

"But she didn't get *inside* you at either of those places. She needs you to be in her home for it to work."

"Give me a break. You're just making shit up now."

"And why would I do that?"

"I don't know. Because you're a freak, because you're a psycho, take your pick."

Logan sat quietly for a moment.

Drew said, "Give me one good reason why I should trust you."

"Because I'm the only one who can save you."

Drew uttered a short, bitter laugh. "You're only interested in saving yourself."

Logan did not attempt to deny the accusation.

It was quiet for a moment. Then Drew said, "Let's say I believe you. Let's say I buy all this crap—she can only get me in my house, on Halloween, at the stroke of midnight, whatever. Let's say I go with you on this, I'm all in. What happens then? If she can't get to me on Halloween inside my house, what happens to her? Does she just vanish in a puff of smoke or something? Will she be gone for good because we tricked her? What are we talking about here? What's the endgame?"

Logan saw no reason for lying at this point. "It's a temporary fix. She'll be gone for a time, but she'll be back. It's her house, and she'll always be there, or at least some part of her will be. And for one month a year, she'll grow progressively stronger until the last day of that month, when her strength peaks . . . and you know the rest."

"So, I'll be safe as long as I stay out of my house on Halloween . . . at least as long as I live there."

"Pretty much."

"And when I move out? What happens then? Does it end with me?"

Logan was silent.

Drew said, "Does it end with me or not?"

Logan looked into Drew's eyes solemnly.

Drew uttered that short, humorless laugh again. "Are you kidding me? This will just go on with the next guy who lives there?" Logan remained silent, but Drew picked up on the unspoken sentiment, and it sent a wave of terror through him. "If my brother stays in that house, will she latch onto him? Is that what you're saying?"

"I'm not saying anything. I don't know what she'll do once you're gone. But I *do* know what she'll do if you're in that house on Halloween night."

"This is *unreal,*" Drew said, shaking his head in frustration and disbelief. "This is completely *unreal.* What have you done here? What the fuck have you *done?*"

Logan waited and then said, "I know it's a lot to process—"

"Process?" Drew said, with a short hysterical laugh. "You think I need to *process?*" Then he lost it. "*This is completely insane. This can't be happening. Shit like this doesn't happen. Not in the real world.*"

Drew's hands were clenched into fists; he looked like he wanted to punch something. Or someone.

Logan spoke calmly. "I know what you're going

through. I thought the same thing when I first saw her. But I got through it, and so will you."

Drew let out a long slow breath, and when he spoke, he was surprised at how calm his voice sounded. "I fucking hate you. Words cannot begin to describe how much I fucking hate you. You pulled me into this with your little bullshit scene, and never once—until I confronted you, of course—never fucking *once* did you have the balls to man up and tell me what was really going on."

"And if I had told you the truth from the beginning, would you have believed me? Without meeting L, without seeing the girls at the amusement park, or the three boys, would you have believed me?"

Drew shook his head, though not in response to Logan's question. "That's not the point, man . . . whether or not I would have believed you isn't the point. The point is," he said, looking into Logan's eyes, "I would have at least had the *choice* to believe you." He paused. "I don't expect someone like you to get that. You're so used to manipulating people, you don't know any better. But if I *had* chosen to believe you, there would have at least been *trust* between us. And that'll take you a lot farther than your bullshit games."

Logan remained silent.

Drew shook his head slowly. "None of that even computes for you, does it? It's beyond your grasp." He smiled sadly, but the disdain still lingered in his eyes. "I'm gonna do what you say, because I *have* to believe you. I have to believe that this isn't just another part of your sick little scene. I have to believe that it's real. I don't have any choice." He shook his head again and sighed. "I don't know. Maybe you are the good guy, and in your own twisted way, you were just trying to help me. I don't know." The sadness faded from his eyes until all that was left was the disdain. "What I do know is that you're a self-absorbed dick, and an all-around asshole."

Logan's expression remained stoic, but Drew thought he saw a flicker in those cool grey eyes, like a flash of silver striking just beneath the surface of that seemingly impenetrable façade.

"Whatever your motive is," Drew said with finality, "it doesn't really matter. I don't trust you, and I don't like you. And if you ever come near me again after this is over, I'll make you wish your dead babysitter *had* killed you."

He held his gaze on Logan for a moment, so that there would be no mistaking the sincerity of his parting statement. Then he got out of the car and walked away.

It could have ended right there. But as Logan had long expected, it did not.

The full moon shone so brightly through his bedroom window that Logan didn't have to turn on the light to locate his phone. It was on the desk where he'd left it earlier, before the sun had gone down and the shadows of All Hallows' Eve had begun to descend in earnest.

There were three voice messages and seven texts. All within the past hour. All from Drew.

Logan scrolled through the texts first.

8:35 PM —CALL ME. IT'S URGENT.

8:51 PM — WHERE ARE YOU? CALL ME.

9:03 PM — WHY WON'T YOU ANSWER YOUR
PHONE? I NEED TO TALK TO YOU RIGHT
NOW.

9:19 PM — I'VE LEFT YOU TWO VOICE MES-
SAGES. PLEASE CALL ME.

9:23 PM — IF YOU'RE STILL MAD AT ME FOR
WHAT I SAID IN THE CAR THE OTHER NIGHT,
I'M SORRY. I WAS PISSED OFF. YOU CAN'T HOLD
THAT AGAINST ME. NOT NOW. PLEASE CALL. I'M
SORRY.

9:27 PM — I CAN'T WAIT ANY LONGER. I HAVE
TO DO SOMETHING. IF YOU DON'T CALL BACK IN
THE NEXT FIVE MINUTES, I'LL GO ON MY OWN.

9:33 PM — MY FUCKING PIECE OF SHIT CAR
WON'T TURN OVER. I'M FUCKING STUCK HERE.
WOULD YOU PLEASE FUCKING CALL ME BEFORE I
GO COMPLETELY FUCKING INSANE!

Logan's heart began to beat a little faster. He played the messages. The first was brief and controlled.

"It's Drew. I need you to call me. Something's happened, and I don't know what to do."

The second was abrupt.

"Call me as soon as you get this."

The third was more detailed. It had been placed at 9:37, and this time, there was no attempt by Drew to mask the desperation in his voice.

"I need you to call me right now. I've sent you a fuckload

of texts already, and I need you to get back to me right now . . . *fuck*. This is no joke, we've got real trouble. My brother . . . my brother is either on his way home or already there. Do you get that? *He's on his way home or already there.* He was supposed to be away for the weekend, but he sent me a text saying he was on his way back *home*."

Drew's voice cut out for a second or two, but the recording continued, and Logan could hear him breathing. Then Drew's voice came back strong.

"He said that he got *my* text and that he was headed back home—but I didn't *send* him a text. *I didn't send him a fucking text.* And now he's on his way home or already there—he might *already fucking be there right now*, and I can't get a hold of you. I'm stuck at my friend's place in Langdon Hills, and no one is here, and my fucking car won't start, and you're not *answering me! I need you to answer me right the fuck now!*"

The line went silent again, and Logan could feel Drew straining on the other end to hold it together. Then Drew's voice came back, quieter, diminished, pleading.

"Please call me. He's going to be all alone in the house with her . . . I'm sorry for what I said to you the other night . . . I'll do anything you want, just please call me."

The message ended there.

Logan looked at the time on his mobile. It was 9:48.

For a second, he tried to make himself believe that it could end here. He tried to listen to the faint voice within, the one that told him he could still save Drew, that he could alter his destiny. But the voice within was merely L, making a long-distance call into a future that had already been set in stone. In that parallel universe where he existed, L was still a kid, filled with hope and dreams for a life that Logan could never have. Logan knew what L could not yet see, because he'd already lived it. Looking at his reflection in the darkened bedroom window, Logan understood that it was far too late to turn back.

He tapped Drew's number on his mobile's little glowing screen. Drew picked up on the first ring.

"My brother is on his way back to the house," he said rapidly. "He may already be there."

"I know," Logan said calmly. "I got your messages."

Drew went on in that same rapid manner: "He sent me a text saying he got my text and that he was headed home, but I didn't *send* him a text, I swear it! I've been trying to contact him, but he doesn't answer. It keeps going to voicemail, and he hasn't answered any of my texts! We need to get to the house *now*."

"I know," Logan said, keeping his voice calm, despite his pounding heart. "You stay put. I'm going over there. I'll call you as soon as I get there."

"NO!" Drew shouted.

"I have to."

"Not without me, you don't. Come get me now."

"I'm not so sure that's a good idea."

Drew snapped. *"Yeah, well, fuck you, he's my brother!"*

Logan hesitated for a second, then said, "Give me the address there."

D rew was waiting at the end of his friend's driveway when Logan's Porsche zoomed up to the curb twenty minutes later. He got in and buckled up, without a word.

They drove in silence for the first several miles. Drew gazed out the window while shaking his leg anxiously.

Logan kept his eyes focused on the road ahead. When Drew asked irritably if they could go any faster, Logan accelerated, without debate.

"I didn't send him a text," Drew said, more to himself than to Logan. "How could he have gotten a text from me if I didn't send him one? I didn't even have my phone on me today. I left it at Matt's place when we went to school this morning." He shook his head, trying to figure it out. "Could she have done it? Is that even possible? You said that ghosts can move things. Could she have gotten to my phone and sent that text? Did she do it to get my brother to come home early? So that I would come to help him? Is that what this is? Or maybe if she couldn't get into my body, she'd just take his? Can she do that? Because we're brothers? Can she just get into his body if I'm not there for her?"

Logan's features remained tight and fixed. He shook his head and said softly, "I don't know. Maybe."

Drew uttered a strained moan. "You've got to be kidding me, man. This can't be happening. You said if I just stayed out of the house, she wouldn't be able to get me. Why didn't you *tell* me that she could get my brother?"

"I don't know that she can," Logan said, keeping his eyes on the road.

"How can you *not* know? You know *everything*. Isn't that your whole deal, knowing everything? *How can you not know?*"

Logan didn't say anything this time. He just punched the accelerator and watched through the windscreen as the Porsche devoured the road ahead.

When he pulled to a stop in his usual spot under the willow across the street from Drew's house—*Marilyn's* house—Logan could almost hear Drew's heartbeat drop to a slow driving throb. The windows were all dark. The house was silent. And parked in the driveway was Jason Thor's Jeep.

Drew felt a hollow thud within as he gazed at the Jeep. They hadn't made it in time. Jason had already arrived and was somewhere inside the house.

Logan said, "Is that his car?"

Drew nodded.

"Are you OK?"

Drew continued to stare at the house in silence.

Logan said, "You don't have to do this. You can just wait for me here—"

But Drew was already out of the car and headed across the street. Logan caught up to him on the porch, where the front door stood ajar. Drew shot a glance at Logan, but Logan's eyes were focused on the space between the door and the jam. With his heart pounding, Drew reached out and pushed the door open.

The foyer was dark.

Drew sniffed and said, "What's that smell?"

Logan didn't respond. Drew reached for the light switch, but when he flipped it, nothing happened.

"*Shit,*" Drew hissed. "Hang on."

He disappeared into the darkness, leaving Logan alone in the foyer, and in the silence that followed, Logan could hear the steady rush of blood drumming at his temples. The last time he'd set foot in this place after nightfall was exactly seven years ago to the date. The skin at the nape of his neck rippled with gooseflesh at the thought, and his legs began to tremble. He was startled by a sudden sound coming from the front closet. The sound of shifting hangers and boxes. Then a snapping sound, and the foyer was lit by the hazy glow of a flashlight. The beam was weak but sufficient enough to cut through the darkness of the foyer.

Drew held the flashlight low and pointed in the direction of the stairs as he called out, "Jay? Jason, are you up there?" When no response came, he said, "He could be asleep, or under the headphones." In his head, he didn't believe either, but his heart still held hope. "Or maybe he went out to look for me. He could be—" He turned the flashlight's beam so that he could see Logan. "What's wrong?"

Logan was trembling, frozen in place, his eyes riveted on the stairs. "Drew, I'm scared to death," he whispered.

A cold chill shot through Drew at the sound of those words coming from Logan. A fear greater than any he'd ever felt in his entire life gripped him, and he whispered back, "Dude, I'm begging you, please don't do this to me. Not now. *Please.*"

Drew's heart was racing madly now because if *Logan* was afraid, there had to be something *beyond* scary waiting up those stairs. He worked hard to hold it together and pushed back against the fear with all his strength.

"It's all right, man, everything is all right. OK?"

"I can't move," Logan whispered through clenched teeth. "I can't go up there."

The fear in Logan's voice cut through Drew's resolve like a sharp blade, but somehow he managed to keep it together.

"No, please, listen," Drew pleaded, "we can do this. But we need to stick together. We'll be all right if we stick together. We gotta have each other's back. OK?"

Logan's response came in a harsh and fearful whisper: *"Drew, you don't know her!"*

Drew froze and stared at Logan with wide eyes. Logan

was trembling fiercely now. A sheen of sweat had broken across his brow, and his face was drained of color. Drew put a hand on Logan's shoulder and squeezed.

"OK. It's gonna be OK. I need you to stay here, though. You wait for me here. I have to go up, man. He's my brother. I'll just go and look—I'll just go and look, and be right back. You just wait for me here, OK? Please, man, he's my brother. I have to go get him. All you have to do is wait here for me, make sure the door stays open, so we can get out, OK?"

Logan nodded, but he was still trembling. "Please hurry. *Please.*"

"I'll be right back," Drew said. He looked into Logan's eyes. "I trust you. Stay by the door and be ready, OK?"

Logan nodded again, and Drew headed for the stairs. He stopped only once, halfway up, when one of the risers creaked and a shadow flitted outside the window in the upstairs hallway. He pointed the dim beam of the flashlight at the window and squinted. There was a cat on the ledge outside. A beautiful black cat with stunning blue eyes. Drew had seen her around before; she'd eaten the food he'd put out for her, but no matter how gently he'd tried to coax her, she'd refused to enter the house. She turned her head now to look inside the window, and her eyes glowed momentarily in the hazy beam of light. She appeared to be gazing directly at Drew as she emitted a low and mournful sound, like a warning. Then she hunkered down, leapt nimbly onto the branch of a tree, and disappeared into the shadows.

Smart girl, Drew thought as he climbed the rest of the stairs.

When he reached the top, he turned the flashlight toward the far end of the hall, and his heart stopped. The door just past the rail that ran half the length of the upstairs hall was open a crack . . . just enough to reveal the faint light that flickered from within.

Drew held his breath for an endless second as he gazed at the thin shaft of light that crept out into the hall. Then he steeled himself and called out his brother's name. When no response came, he took a step forward. And then another, and another, until he was standing in front of the door. With his heart beating like a great drum inside his chest, Drew pressed his fingertips to the door and pushed it open. As it swung soundlessly on its hinges, the memory of L's warning that night a few weeks ago flooded his consciousness with chilling clarity . . .

The oldest boy is dangerous. He's more afraid of you than you are of him because he knows that you're stronger. But you have to stay away from him. Promise that you won't go to the candleroom.

Despite this warning, Drew crossed the threshold, some distant part of him knowing that it was already too late to turn back.

The room was arranged like the set of a play, lit by countless candles, whose flickering tips bathed the horrifying scene in a paradoxically warm golden glow. Along the walls, words had been scrawled in giant red letters that dripped like paint. But Drew understood that this was not paint. Stark angry words that stood out like accusations: CUNTLICKER . . . APPLE-POLISHER . . . WHOREMONGER . . . BITCH!

But it wasn't the words that held Drew's attention—he was only peripherally aware of these. It was the figure at the center of the scene: the still and silent figure of his older brother, Jason. Stripped naked and down on his knees, hands bound behind his back, eyes staring upward, a shiny red apple wedged between his teeth, a hunting knife buried to the hilt in his stomach.

Drew stood in a trancelike stupor, unable to move, as the eerie tableau of candles and blood seemed to float toward him in slow motion.

A t the same time, down in the darkened foyer, Logan was trembling fiercely as memory upon memory came crashing down upon him . . .

Martyn, bound and naked on his knees, candles burning all around him; Marilyn holding out the ripe red apple, telling him to take a bite; their lips touching as juice from the apple spilled down Martyn's chin; her soft and delicate hands running through Martyn's dark, silky hair; a drop of blood spilling from Martyn's lip where she'd bit him—a love bite—and then more kissing, deep and passionate, as he, Logan (L—he was L back then), watched from the shadows of the hallway, paralyzed . . . until she'd called to him, telling him not to be afraid, that it was just a scene that she and Martyn were playing out, and would he like to join them? His little body had been trembling so fiercely that he'd thought he might faint. But he hadn't fainted. He'd stood there trembling while music spilled softly from the stereo—*Three Imaginary Boys*—and the scene in the candleroom floated toward him.

And he could hear the music now, as he moved from the foyer to the foot of the stairs. He could hear that old song coming from the stereo up in the bedroom—the *candleroom*. It drifted down the stairs and grew stronger with each step he mounted. He could feel it thrumming in his blood, echoing in each heartbeat, calling him up to that room at the top. And as he ascended the stairs, he did not dare look back, for fear that he would see the steps behind him disappearing into oblivion.

U P in the bedroom, Drew remained frozen in place, his gaze still locked on the lifeless figure of his older brother. He was distantly aware of a voice calling out to him, but he could not turn away from the grisly sight. The voice sounded like Logan's, but there was something different in the tone: a desperate, pleading timbre that was so very unlike the Logan he knew. It came in a harsh whisper, filled with the fear of a child.

"*Drew . . . Drew!*"

Calling as if from a great distance.

"*Drew, please . . .*"

Closer now, but still distant.

"*Drew, let's go!*"

Then, no longer distant but calling from the hallway just outside the bedroom.

"*Drew, let's go now!*"

A creaking floorboard, a shaky breath at the nape of his neck, and Drew understood that he was no longer alone. Still, he did not turn around.

Then, from directly in front of him, there came a sudden sound—a sickening sucking sound, like a blade being yanked from a wet side of beef.

Drew remained frozen, gazing down at the grotesque statue of his brother's corpse. But something was different now. Something had changed. The hunting knife that had been buried in his brother's stomach was no longer there. Just a jagged gaping wound where it had been.

"*Drew . . . Drew!*" Logan called out in that harsh whisper again—only this time the tone of voice sounded more like the Logan he knew. And this time, that tone sent a wave of pure terror through him. "*Drew, she's here!*"

A hand dropped onto Drew's shoulder from behind and pulled hard, spinning him around so that he was face to face with Logan.

"*She's here!*" Logan screamed.

At first, Drew looked like a sleepwalker, dazed and confused. Then recognition dawned, and a single tear spilled down his cheek. As he gazed into Logan's eyes, which no longer looked grey but a stark, shining silver, he was dimly aware that the two of them were not alone in the room.

Logan was trembling uncontrollably as he screamed again, "*She's here! She's here!*" But it wasn't until he pulled Drew closer that the truth dawned. Logan wasn't trembling with *fear*; he was trembling with *rage*.

Drew felt suddenly cold when Logan pulled him close enough that their noses were almost touching and growled, "*She's here!*"

Drew stared into Logan's silver eyes in stupefied wonder . . . until his brain caught up with the signal that his body was sending out, and a burning pain exploded in his stomach. He reached up with a clumsy hand and felt Logan's gloved fist wrapped tightly around the handle of the hunting knife that now protruded from his stomach.

Logan drove the blade in deeper as he pulled Drew closer and snarled, "*Did you think I would let you have her? Did you honestly think I would stand by and let you and your brother have her? Did you think I would tolerate even the thought of the two of you touching her? Fucking her? Did you think I'd let you get away with it? Did you think that I would show you any more mercy than I showed my own brother? Did you?"* He drove the blade of the knife deeper into Drew's stomach. *"Did you really think I would sit by and let you have that cuntlicking little two-timing bitch? Did you think that I'd let you live here with her and fuck her without any consequences, you whoremongering apple-polishing smug jock prick!"*

Logan released his grip on the knife's handle, and Drew fell to his knees, gasping, as blood began to fill his lungs.

"You really should have listened to the brat," Logan said, panting heavily. "He came to warn you about me. He even tried to work on me through the old memory high-way, placing doubt and guilt into my thoughts—clever little fucker, he actually had me thinking that I *wanted* to save you . . . right up until the very end. But then he doesn't know *half* the shit I do, does he?"

Logan looked at his reflection in the darkened window, and his eyes shone silver. Drew coughed a runner of blood onto the floor.

"Poor little L. He's been here since earlier today, when I came to settle up with your brother—that would be after I dropped your mobile off at your friend's place . . . which would be after I sent the text to big brother here. I nicked it from your pocket that night in my car. You really should keep a better eye on your things."

He turned away from Drew and aimed his fiery gaze at the small figure standing in the hallway just outside the open door. "And *you* should never have tried to fuck with me, little man."

Through blurred vision, Drew could see L, and he understood now that it hadn't been Logan calling out to him in that desperate pleading whisper moments ago. It had been L. He had come to save Drew. He had come to save him from the oldest of the three boys, the one he had warned Drew to stay away from. And now L stood alone and trembling in the hall, with tears in his eyes. Drew wanted to go to him, to hold him in his arms and tell him that it was all right. But he could scarcely breathe, let alone move. All he could do was watch and wait until it was over. And by the coldness he felt creeping over his body, it wouldn't be long.

"Do you see what you've done?" Logan shouted at the boy. *"Did you really think you could defeat me? Did you think you could save him? Your brave and loyal knight! Look at him!"*

Hot tears spilled down L's cheeks as he looked at Drew.

"I've done this for you," Logan screamed.

L shook his head.

"Yes, you ungrateful little bastard. I've done all this for you because we are one and the same, you and I. Everything I do is for us. And you—you traitorous little whiny bitch—have tried to fuck me over at every turn. You keep laboring under the delusion that you *control* me *when it's the other way around:* I *control* you! *I'm the one who did all of this. I set the scene. I tell the players where to move and what to say. Your little attempt to rewrite my story has had zero effect. I control everything. You, me, him, her! Everything! I control all you see and beyond because I am Zeus All-Fucking-Mighty, and* anyone *who attempts to fuck me will be met with swift vengeance and furious wrath!"*

Logan moved fast at the boy and crouched down so that they were eye to eye. L flinched, but he didn't run.

"Take a good look into these eyes, little man," Logan said in a low and deadly tone, "and tell me that I'm lying."

Their gazes locked for an infinite moment. Then a slow smile broke out at one corner of Logan's mouth as that familiar look of defiance crept into L's solemn grey eyes.

"You really are clueless, aren't you, champ?" Logan said, with an arched brow.

L remained stoic. Logan's smile deepened.

"You still think it was *her*," Logan said, with a curious glint in his eye. "You still think that dear sweet Marilyn got inside your little head and told you to stab her that night, don't you. You actually *believe* that she could mastermind a brilliant climax like that." He snorted a short, indignant laugh. "She wouldn't have had the courage, let alone the creativity, to execute such an exquisite plan. She's a clever witch and has knowledge, but not half as clever as the pupil she passed that knowledge on to. That would be *you*, little man . . . and by extension, me."

Logan grinned, almost proudly, at the look of suspicion in L's eyes.

"It's true. How do you think you've been able to cross over into this universe? Nifty little trick, eh? You're much more powerful than you imagine." He paused, and his silver eyes shone darkly. "But you're not as powerful as I. And you never will be. I'll always be several steps ahead of you."

L's small chest rose and fell rapidly now, but he held his gaze, determined not to show Logan his fear.

"*She* didn't make you do anything that night," Logan said. "And deep down, you know it."

L shook his head, and Logan smiled as he read the kid's thoughts like a book.

"Oh, it wasn't *you*, either, champ. Yes, it may have been your little hand that wielded the knife, but it was *me* in the here and now pulling your strings, Pinocchio." Once again, his eyes shone dark and deadly serious. *"I'm* the one who told you to do it. It was *my* voice you heard whispering inside your head."

L could not conceal the shock in his eyes, and for a flicker of a second, this pleased Logan. Then his gaze went dark again.

"I was going to have you stab Martyn too—I wanted more than anything to look through your eyes and see the life drain out of him. I wanted him to see *me* in you and know who it really was that was sending him off. But you fucked that one when you ran and locked yourself in the closet like a little chickenshit bitch. All that blood freaked you out, and I couldn't get back inside your hysterical little brain." He shook his head, with a sad smile. "But I had fore-seen that possibility—that's why I had you send that first text to the police, well before the madness got underway. Always have a contingency plan.

"Of course, Martyn really helped things along when he lost it and started stabbing at the door like a wild man. And let me assure you of something, kiddo, he wasn't trying to save you from the scary ghost in the closet. If the police hadn't got there in time and shot him dead, Martyn, our beloved older brother, would have killed you in a fit of rage—*that's* how powerful that cunning little bitch's grasp on him was. He loved her more than you, and he would have killed you—and in turn, me—if not for my quick thinking and thorough planning." His eyes brimmed with sudden tears, but his anger kept them from falling. "In *this* universe, he left you for her. They moved away and had a baby—can you imagine how fucked up that kid would have been?" He chuckled bitterly, and his eyes lit with a fiery passion. "*I* saved us both that night. I changed the course of the *future*. I did it for *us*, so *you* should be a little more grateful."

Across the room, Drew coughed up a small pool of blood as he struggled to get up.

Logan smiled and shook his head, keeping his gaze focused on L. "He's strong. His brother Jason went out like a light, but he's strong." He paused, and that strange smile of pride crossed his lips again. "You must have made quite an impression on him, L—he still thinks you're worth saving. He doesn't understand that all roads for *you* lead to *me*."

L's heart pounded a slow drumbeat as he gazed at Drew. He struggled valiantly to hold back tears, but when Drew rose painfully up to his knees and looked at him, the tears began to fall again. Logan closed his eyes and sighed. When he opened them, he didn't look angry. He put a gentle hand on L's cheek and brushed the tears away with his thumb.

"I know that you want to believe in him," Logan said softly, "but trust me, he's like Martyn. Eventually, he would have left us, too. If not for her, then some other whore. He's not the hero. In real life—as well as in death—there are no heroes."

L stood firm, his gaze focused, obstinate. For a second Logan was tempted to slap that defiant look off the boy's face, but secretly he felt a swelling of pride. Any other little kid would have turned tail and run from a guy as transparently crazy and dangerous as Logan. But then L wasn't any other little kid. He was Logan before there *was* a Logan. Before the corruption of innocence.

Logan's gaze softened. He nodded his forehead against L's, while gently squeezing the back of the boy's neck.

"I'm going to do this for you," Logan whispered. "But I make no promises, do you understand? If he breaks your heart—and they always do—you can't come running back to me. You don't belong here. This is *my* time, and you don't belong here. Do you understand?"

L nodded as fresh tears spilled down his cheeks.

Logan rose and walked over to Drew. He squatted and, with his lips close to Drew's ear, spoke in a soft and reasonable tone. "You have a choice now, which is more than most ever get in this fucked up world. But know that once you make this choice, there is no turning back." He paused and glanced at L before going on. "You can stay here with the whore in your little love nest, or you can go with L." He paused again and then added a third option. "*Or* you can leave them both behind, like Martyn did . . . like your own brother did when I liberated him from his mortal coil a few hours ago."

Drew coughed hard through gritted teeth, a sudden surge of anger welling within him. Logan smiled pleasantly.

"I'm guessing you'll go with door number three," Logan said confidentially. "But in any case, it's time to bring down the curtain on the third act."

Logan patted Drew's shoulder and stood up. L saw what he was about to do and cried out. But it was too late. Logan raised one foot and brought it down hard on Drew's back, driving him face-first to the floor. There was a sharp cracking sound as the handle of the hunting knife hit the floor, and the blade was driven deeper into Drew's stomach. A quick spasm followed. And then Drew lay still and silent, a thin line of fresh blood running from one corner of his mouth, his dead eyes staring at the small boy in the doorway.

L tried to run to Drew, but a set of cold hands suddenly settled on his shoulders and held him back.

Logan looked up from Drew's corpse and smiled at the teenage girl who now stood behind L. She looked as real as she had the last time he'd seen her alive—in this very room exactly seven years ago. Though her gaze was firmly fixed in his direction, she was not looking at Logan. She was looking at the newly minted apparition of the tall and muscular blond guy standing at Logan's side. And the flame of passion in her lovely eyes was clear to see.

Drew was still looking down at his bloody and mangled body in a sort of dazed wonder when Logan said, "I know it must be eternally fascinating to look upon your own corpse, but the clock is ticking, and we really need to move things along here." He paused briefly and then said, "Time to choose, hero—the brat, the bitch, or your freedom. Which will it be?"

Drew looked up. First at Logan, then at the small boy and the teenage girl standing in the doorway.

Logan glanced at his fingernails with casual aplomb as he spoke in a sing-song manner: "Tick-tock . . . tick-tock."

Drew's hands momentarily clenched into fists at his sides and then relaxed when he looked toward the doorway again. He wanted nothing more to do with Logan. He was only concerned with the sight that lay before him. He knew what he wanted more than anything now, and that was all that mattered.

He looked directly into Marilyn's eyes as he approached the doorway. They were as lovely and alluring as he remembered from the times he'd seen her before—at the swim meet in New Lennox . . . on that crisp night at the amusement park . . . in the depths of his dreams, where she had touched him in places and ways that had thrilled and excited him beyond belief. He understood how easy it must have been for Logan and Martyn to fall under her spell and not want to come up for air. His own desire for her, particularly at this moment when she seemed to glow from within, was nearly insurmountable. She was, without exception, the most beautiful girl he'd ever set eyes on.

You know you like it.

As those words emanated from Marilyn's soul, Drew could feel Logan tensing behind him. But he wasn't afraid of Logan. What more could Logan possibly do to him now that Drew was already dead? In death, he was beyond Logan's reach, and Logan knew it. He could take this beautiful girl into his embrace and have her right here and now, and there would be nothing Logan could do about it—short of taking his own life . . . and *that* was something Logan's monumental ego would never allow.

For a moment, Drew imagined what the scene would be like—he and Marilyn in the throes of passion, while Logan looked on in impotent fury. Part of Drew relished the thought of Logan suffering in such a manner. But another part—the part that was ruled by rational cognition—knew better. Logan possessed an undeniable power—certainly beyond that of L, and possibly even greater than the otherworldly sway of Marilyn herself. He had orchestrated this entire three-act horror show, manipulating all of the players, both living and dead, into his grand finale, with scarcely a hitch. And he'd set all of this into motion by reaching across the divide between parallel universes to implant a single thought in the consciousness of his unwitting ten-year-old self. In a whispered breath across that chasm of space and time, Logan had rewritten history.

Drew looked over his shoulder at Logan and spoke without parting his lips: *You can't get to me anymore, because I'm dead, and you have no real power over the dead, do you? That's why you needed me to do your little scene, isn't it? You needed a living person as bait to draw her out. And when you discovered that I was living in her house, you started parking outside across the street, watching through the window, waiting for her to show up. And when she did show up, you realized that you still had no power over her. You can't get to her because she's dead, and you can't control the dead, can you? With all your cunning and power, you can't get to either of us now.*

Something shifted in Drew's eyes then, like a tiny spark igniting a flame.

But you can *still get to L. He's only an imprint here, but in his own universe, he's as real as you are, isn't that what you told me? He's a living kid with his whole life ahead of him. He still has a chance not to become you. It's true, isn't it? In one of those infinite parallel universes that you mentioned, L still has the chance not to become you.*

Logan gazed at Drew with those canny silver eyes, as if to acknowledge that they were indeed on the same page. With someone there to watch over him and guide him, L had the opportunity to travel a very different path than one Logan had chosen in this divergent universe.

Drew turned back to the doorway, where Marilyn stood with her hands still resting on L's skinny shoulders. But he scarcely acknowledged Marilyn with a glance. He bent down to one knee, looked directly into L's eyes, and said aloud, "I'm still here. I'm not going anywhere."

Fresh tears welled in the boy's eyes. He broke from

Marilyn's grasp and ran to Drew, who scooped him up into his arms and held him close, whispering, "I'm still here."

Across the room, Logan stood silent, steeling himself against an unexpected wave of emotion. It took a moment, but he crushed it from within, and when he turned his gaze to Marilyn, his silver eyes shone darkly once again, as if to assure her that he had indeed arrived at the final stage of his development.

I am now the boy you predicted I would one day become.

He thought he saw a minute flicker of fear in her eyes, but it might have just been a trick of the wavering candlelight. In any case, it didn't matter. She would soon know fear intimately. He wasn't done with her yet.

Drew rose, with L in his arms, and turned to face Logan. The boy clung tightly to him, his head resting on Drew's shoulder.

Marilyn took a step forward.

Logan snapped his fingers and pointed at her. "*You* don't get to have him," he said sharply, freezing her in her tracks. "The brat can take one over with him, and it appears he's chosen wisely."

Logan turned his rigid finger toward the window wall and, with a facile gesture, created a tear in the fabric of time. Marilyn's expression remained composed, but Logan could tell that she was impressed. He kept a guarded eye on her as he spoke to Drew.

"That's your window, old sport. Don't bother trying to remember the path back here—I'll have already erased it by the time you get the little tiger home and tucked safely into bed." He shot a steely gaze at Drew. "You two stay on your side of the divide, and I'll stay on mine. I have no intention of fucking with either of you, and I truly wish you both the best in your new life together. See to it that you extend me the same courtesy . . . I won't be nearly as gracious should we happen to cross paths again."

Drew didn't respond. There was no need to. The only thing he wanted now was to get L as far away from here as possible. He looked at the tear in the wall. The edges glowed like smoldering cinders as if the opening had been carved out by a blowtorch. He bent down, protecting L, as he stepped through the opening that led to the path on the other side.

It was still nighttime, and the air was brisk, but the chill that had permeated the bedroom from which they'd just come was absent. All Drew could feel was the warmth generating from the boy who now slept soundly in his arms, and this was more than enough to keep him going all the way home.

As the glowing tear in the wall, through which Drew and L had just departed, became a solid surface once again, Logan stood silent, with his back to the doorway. He didn't have to turn around and look to know that she was still there. He could *feel* her presence. And he could read her thoughts. They were connected, he and Marilyn. They always had been. Even when she'd chosen Martyn over him, he'd known in his heart that she was and always would be his and his alone. It had taken time to master the craft she'd taught him, but eventually he'd managed to do it. Nothing could sever the bond between them. Not even death.

But that didn't mean she would stop trying.

She was still angry at him for killing her—which,

Logan reckoned, was completely understandable—and she wanted him to pay for it. When she'd violated Drew in his sleep the other night, she'd enjoyed knowing that Logan was watching from his car across the street. When she'd climbed out from inside of Drew after and floated at the window, there had been real fire in her eyes. And that hadn't been the first time. Logan had looked through that window on other nights and seen her inside with Drew— and once even with Drew's older brother Jason. And she'd enjoyed it every time. She'd enjoyed shoving his nose in her debauchery with the Thor brothers. Taunting him. Daring him to come in and stop her.

And tonight he'd finally done just that. He'd stopped her dead in her tracks.

Tonight he'd shown her the extent of his power and the depth of his devotion by bringing down the curtain on her little peep show once and for all.

But it wasn't over yet.

There was still one thing left to do. An encore, of sorts. A real show-stopper. A little something to bring down not only the curtain but the entire house. Because as long as she remained in this house, she would be completely free to continue her pursuits of pleasure and torment.

Logan turned to the doorway, and though Marilyn was no longer standing there, he could feel her presence.

She's here . . . she's here!

Logan smiled bitterly and thought: *But not for long.*

Then he reached out and tipped over one of the candles. It fell to the floor at the side of the bed and kissed the dust ruffle with its flame. And as the fire crawled along the duvet and up to the pillows, Logan knocked over more candles.

He stood in the doorway for a moment, calmly watching as the flames licked the walls and consumed the drapes. Then he backed out into the hallway and casually strode to the stairs—which, contrary to the lyrics of Marilyn's favorite song, had not disappeared.

By the time he reached the bottom of the stairs, the fire had already crept out into the upstairs hallway. He carried with him two candles from the bedroom. He tossed one into the living room and the other into the dining room—he'd doused both with kerosene after he'd taken care of business with Drew's older brother earlier. And as he watched from the foyer, the flames caught on nicely.

He stepped outside and headed down the front path at a casual pace, and only looked back once he was inside his car across the street.

The living room walls were crawling with flames now, and by that raging light, he could see Marilyn standing at the picture window, gazing out at him. She was so beautiful, it almost hurt to look at her. And soon he would be able to look at her anytime he pleased. Indeed, he would have her all to himself, for within a short time her entire house would be reduced to nothing more than a smoldering pile of ash and rubble—and they both knew that there was only one other house that would have her . . . the only other house where she'd ever truly felt at home.

Logan's silver eyes shone in triumph as he gazed upon her flaming countenance through the window and projected one last thought: *I'll be waiting for you up in Martyn's old room, my love—we'll celebrate your homecoming with a special scene I've been working on just for you.*

And with that, he fired up the Porsche's engine and drove off into the night.